The Saga of ERIK the VIKING

TERRY JONES
MICHAEL FOREMAN

PAVILION

FOREWORD

THIS BOOK IS THE RESULT of my dissatisfaction with the Icelandic Sagas the first time I read them. I expected them to be tales of wonder and adventure, full of weird monsters and demons roaming the Earth in search of mortals to destroy! I thought they would be full of fantasy and invention and flights of the imagination.

The first Icelandic saga I read was the *Njal's Saga*, and found it, on first reading, to be a rather pedestrian account of family feuds. How somebody stole another farmer's chicken, and how that farmer then stole the first farmer's cow, and how the first farmer then stole the second farmer's horse, and how the second farmer then murdered the first farmer's child, or wife or near relative. (I am parodying, of course.)

Moreover the *Njal's Saga* is full of passages like this: 'A man named Hoskuld lived there, the son of Dala-Koll (Koll from the Dalir district). His mother was Thorgerd, the daughter of Thorstein the Red, who was the son of Olaf the White, whose father was Ingjald Helgason. Ingjald's mother was Thora, the daughter of Sigurd Snake-in-the-eye, who was the son of Ragnar Shaggy-breeches. Thorstein the Red's mother was Unn the Deep-minded; she was the daughter of Ketil Flat-nose, who was the son of Bjorn Buna. Hoskuld lived at Hoskuldsstadir in the valley of Laxardal…' and so on. I found it hard to get past such passages.

We eventually parodied the *Njal's Saga* in an episode of *Monty Python* called *Njorl's Saga*. Erik Njorl can't mount his horse because of a Voice that is constantly reading out the endless list of lineages. The saga eventually gets taken over by the North Malden Mayor's Office, thinly disguised as the North Malden Icelandic Saga Society, trying to attract business and investment to North Malden.

★

In 1979, I had written a book called *Fairy Tales* for my daughter, Sally, when she was five. When my son, Bill, reached five, I obviously had to write a book for him. We had just visited an exhibition of Vikings at the British Museum, so I asked Bill if he would like a story about Vikings and he said yes. This gave me the chance to write the Sagas as I would have liked them to have been: full of flights of the imagination and adventurous exploits, monsters and creatures and magic and fantasy.

Although, since then, I have changed my mind about the Icelandic Sagas. I was given *The Complete Sagas of The Icelanders* in five volumes, and have found them to be really fascinating. The tales are, indeed, told in a prosaic way, but they are fascinating *because* of this. They are glimpses of lives lived seven hundred to a thousand years ago without the artifice of plot or the adornments of rhetoric. Lives, moreover, lived on the margins of civilization, that show people to have been just as noble and virtuous, devious and cunning as any people are today. The Icelandic Sagas show us that we human beings are the same the world over and whatever age we live in. Thank goodness.

Terry Jones
March 2013

CONTENTS

ERIK AND THE STORM

THIS IS THE TALE of a Viking warrior who lived hundreds and hundreds of years ago. His name was Erik. His ship was called Golden Dragon, and its figurehead was a fierce monster carved out of wood, and covered with gold leaf.

One day Erik said to his wife, 'I must find the land where the sun goes at night.' But his wife replied, 'No one has ever been to that far country. And of those who have tried few have ever returned.'

'You are right,' said Erik, 'but, until I have sought that distant land, I shall never sleep in my bed again.'

So he called his son, who was fifteen years old, and told him he must guard their home by day and night. Then he took his sword, which was called Blueblade, stepped on board Golden Dragon and sailed off towards the setting sun.

That night they sailed on far from land, and Erik stood at the helm of Golden Dragon, gazing into the darkness. Erik's men whispered to each other that they were seeking the land where the sun goes at night, and that no one had ever found it and lived to tell the tale.

Just then a bright green light appeared above them, and a star shaped like a dragon leapt across the sky. Erik turned to his men and said, 'We shall find what we seek.' And no one dared say a word after that.

The next morning they found themselves alone on the ocean with great waves heaving the ship up and down. Erik looked up into the sky and smelt the wind.

'We shan't make it!' whispered Erik's men, one to the other, as the storm clouds blotted out the sun.

'We'll be wrecked at sea,' they murmured as the first drops of rain fell on the deck.

'There's land!' called out Erik. 'Take down the sails … we'll have to row for it.'

They leant on their oars as the rain began to pour down on them. And the speck of land on the horizon got bigger as the skies got darker and the sea grew rougher.

But they rowed with all their might and all their main, and, as the lightning forked across the heavens and the thunder rolled all round them, they got closer and closer to land.

'Rocks to port!' cried the look-out, and the helmsman steered Golden Dragon round to starboard. 'Rocks to starboard!' cried the look-out, and Golden Dragon swung back to port again. 'Look out ahead!' cried Erik, and the golden monster on the helm scraped against the rocks as the sea dragged them down and then threw them up again.

'We've had it now!' cried Erik's men one to the other and they shut their eyes.

'Keep rowing!' cried out Erik, and he steered the ship between the rocks and the boiling sea until all at once they found themselves in a deep fjord.

One by one Erik's men opened their eyes. The rain still poured down on them and the lightning lit up the wild rocks above them, but the water was calm and they were safe.

'Now we must sleep,' said Erik. 'But tomorrow we shall repair Golden Dragon before we dare go back on the high seas.'

His men laid the mast down and threw the sails across it like a tent, and there they slept for the rest of that stormy night.

ERiK AND THE ENCHANTRESS OF THE FJORD

THE NEXT DAY they set to work to repair Golden Dragon. But Erik took three of his best hunters and said, 'We shall kill some wild boar and tonight we shall feast.' Erik and Ragnar Forkbeard and Sven the Strong and Thorkhild set off into the wild forest.

They had not gone more than a mile before they came to a cave. At the entrance to the cave was a strange creature, half bird and half wolf.

'Erik!' said the creature, and its voice sounded like a thousand voices speaking together, 'my mistress is waiting for you,' and it pointed into the gloomy cave.

'Who is your mistress?' asked Erik.

'She who will tell you what you want to know,' replied the creature.

But Ragnar Forkbeard gripped Erik by the arm. 'Do not go into that dark cave. For I fear you will never come out again.'

'I must,' said Erik.

But Sven the Strong gripped Erik by the other arm. 'If you are killed we are all lost,' he said.

'I must find out what I want to know,' said Erik.

And then Thorkhild stood in front of him and said, 'Perhaps she is the Enchantress of the Fjord who never lets any man return?'

'If she can tell me what I want to know,' replied Erik, 'I must meet her.'

Then he strode into the cave, and the other three would have followed him but the strange creature, half bird, half wolf, barred their way with its great talons, and bared its wolf teeth. Whereupon Ragnar Forkbeard and Thorkhild and Sven the Strong drew their swords and advanced towards it as one.

Meanwhile Erik walked boldly through the cave, and the light from the entrance got dimmer and dimmer until there was no light at all, and Erik was feeling his way along the rocky walls of the cave.

11

Suddenly he stopped dead in his tracks. Above his head he could hear a sound like someone breathing. He looked up, but he could see nothing. 'Who's there?' he cried.

'Go deeper into the cave,' said a voice ... and it sounded like his mother, although she was many, many miles away in another land.

Erik put his hand on his sword and went deeper into the cave. Suddenly he stopped, for he could hear another sound above him. It sounded like a heart beating.

'Who's there?' he cried.

'You must go deeper into the cave,' said a voice ... and it sounded like his father, although he had been dead for many years.

But Erik pulled his helmet more firmly onto his head and went deeper into the cave.

And as he got deeper, the cave grew warmer and he saw a red glow ahead of him. And as he got nearer and nearer he let go of his sword and took off his helmet and he found himself in a small room. It was warm and soft and on the floor had been laid out food and drink and a straw bed. Erik was overcome by a desire to lie down and go to sleep, but something inside him told him to beware.

'Rest yourself,' said his father's voice.

'I cannot,' said Erik, 'for my men are waiting for me to return.'

'Sleep my child,' said his mother's voice.

'I should like to ...' said Erik, and he lay down on the straw bed, but still something inside him told him to beware.

'I seek she who will tell me what I want to know ...' he said, and his eyes were half closing with sleep.

'This is all you need to know,' said a soft voice at his ear, and he turned and saw a young girl beside him whose skin was green as jade. She held up a golden charm on a golden chain, and said, 'Here, wear this around your neck and you will know everything you need to know,' and she lifted it up and Erik looked at her eyes, and still something inside him told him to beware. But he bent his head, and the beautiful green girl placed the chain over his head, and a voice inside him said, 'Stop! Before it's too late,' but the chain was already around his neck and resting on his shoulders.

The green girl gave a cruel laugh, and Erik's mind went suddenly clear like the water in the stream, and he suddenly knew that this was the Enchantress of the Fjord, and that

no man ever returns from her embrace and that now he knew all he needed to know. But the chain was round his neck, and he realised that although his mind was clear he could not move a single muscle.

'You fool!' cried the green Enchantress, who now looked a million years old. 'How could anyone tell you what you wanted to know when you yourself didn't even know what it was you wanted to ask!'

And she took a great iron stake and was just about to drive it through the golden chain to fix it to the wall when there was a shout and a blaze of light and there stood Ragnar Forkbeard and Sven the Strong and Thorkhild, torn and stained with the bright green blood of the wolf-bird, but safe and holding flaming torches in their hands.

For a moment Erik was blinded by the light and the Enchantress of the Fjord was too, but in that time, Ragnar Forkbeard saw the chain round Erik's neck and knew what it was. So he snatched it off and before the green Enchantress could do anything, he had thrown it over her neck; she froze as solid and as still as Erik had been, and by the look in her eyes, they could see that she knew everything she needed to know.

Erik and Ragnar Forkbeard and Sven the Strong and Thorkhild ran from that place as fast as they could, but as they reached the mouth of the cave, they saw to their horror the

carcass of the wolf-bird, lying where it had fallen in a pool of green blood, suddenly rear up and block their way. Before they had time to draw their swords again, it spoke and its thousand voices were like distant echoes calling from another world.

'Erik!' they said. 'We are the spirits of others like you who did not know the question to which we sought the answer, and so were ensnared by the Green Enchantress. But now you and your comrades have set us free.'

And with that the creature seemed to collapse upon itself and split up into a thousand different shapes that fluttered up into the sky and were gone, like moths to the sun.

Then Sven the Strong sealed up the mouth of the cave with great boulders and rocks, and they all went back to their ship.

ERIK AND THE SEA DRAGON

WHEN THE SHIP, Golden Dragon, had been repaired, Erik and his men dragged her back into the water and held a feast.

Then they sailed off into the uncharted seas.

When they had been travelling three days and three nights they entered a thick mist, and could see neither to right nor left nor in front nor behind.

Thorkhild came to Erik and said, 'There is something strange about this mist.'

'You are right,' replied Erik. 'Mist is always whitey grey, but this is sometimes red, sometimes blue.'

'But the strangest thing about it,' said Thorkhild, 'is that it is warm. Whereas mist is always cold and damp.'

So Erik stood in front of his men and said, 'Has any one of you ever seen such a mist as this?' But they all shook their heads.

Just then they heard the most terrible clap of thunder right over their heads, and the whole boat shook with the sound, and the men trembled as the thunder rolled on and on above them.

Thorkhild looked at Erik and said, 'There is something strange about this thunder.'

'You are right,' replied Erik. 'Thunder always follows the lightning and yet we have had no lightning.'

'But the strangest thing about it,' said Thorkhild, 'is that it does not stop but gets louder and louder, whereas thunder always dies away.'

At that moment Sven the Strong pointed up into the sky and said, 'Look! The sun!' And they all looked up through the mist and saw a great light shining through at them. And Thorkhild turned to Erik and said, 'If that is indeed the sun, it is a very strange sun.'

And Erik said, 'You are right. I have never seen the sun with a black spot right in the middle like that, nor have I seen the sun moving through the sky first one way and then the other.'

'But the strangest thing about it,' said Thorkhild, 'is that I have only ever seen one sun in the heavens, but now I see two!'

And at that a great cry went up from all on board: 'It's the Great Dragon of the North Sea!' they cried. 'Those suns are its eyes!' said Erik.

'And that thunder is its roar!' said Thorkhild, and at that moment they saw its huge jaws and they saw that the mist was not mist at all, but the smoke that issued from its fiery nostrils.

'We are lost!' cried Erik's men. 'Nothing can save us now!'

But Erik said, 'To the oars! We must row as we have never rowed before!' And they leapt to the oars, but try as they might they could not escape, for the Dragon of the North Sea opened its mouth and began to suck the waters down its great fiery throat, and the ship was carried back twice as fast as they could row forwards.

When Erik saw it was no good and that the Sea Dragon was upon them, he turned to Ragnar Forkbeard and said, 'What shall we do?'

Ragnar Forkbeard did not answer but, white as a sheet, he ran to the sleeping quarters.

'Has it come to this,' asked Erik, 'that Ragnar Forkbeard has lost his courage and his tongue?' And as he spoke the Sea Dragon loomed above the ship and a jet of flame licked across the deck, and the men ran here and there putting out fires.

Just then Ragnar Forkbeard reappeared carrying two bolsters and he said, 'I have lost neither my courage nor my tongue.'

And with that he strapped the bolsters on his back and started to climb the mast.

Sven the Strong turned to Erik and said, 'Ragnar Forkbeard has not lost his courage or his tongue – he has lost his wits.' Just then they heard a fearful noise and they span round to see the great Sea Dragon take the stern post in its mouth and snap it in two with its teeth.

Erik lifted his spear and threw it with all his might at the great Dragon, but it just glanced off its horny skin. Then Thorkhild threw his great spear, but that clattered to the deck without piercing the Sea Dragon. Then Sven the Strong stood up, raised his spear, and threw it with every ounce of strength he had, and the shaft went straight and true and entered the creature in the soft skin above its lip. For a moment the Sea Dragon drew back, but not for long, and its great jaws closed around the after-deck and Erik's men all ran back in their fear.

'We've had it now!' said Sven the Strong, but Erik pointed up in the air. And they all looked in amazement at the top of the mast. For there was Ragnar Forkbeard, clinging on by his legs, with a bolster in each hand.

The Sea Dragon took another great bite, and half the boat was between its fierce jaws, and its eyes were on a level with the mast-top and its nostrils were thrust into the sails. Whereupon Ragnar Forkbeard leapt onto its nose and gave a most tremendous shout that made everyone look up, and even the Dragon paused and tried to focus its eyes on the tiny figure on its nose. Then Ragnar Forkbeard took one bolster and plunged it into the Dragon's right nostril, and the second into its left nostril. The Dragon paused again. Then Ragnar Forkbeard took his good sword and plunged it into the two bolsters – one after the other – so that they opened up and all the feathers billowed into the air as the Dragon breathed out, and then as it breathed in again, all the feathers suddenly disappeared – sucked into its nostrils.

The Dragon paused, and its jaws went slack, and Ragnar Forkbeard jumped for his life just as the Dragon sneezed a most almighty sneeze, and the sails of the ship filled and the ship shot out of the Dragon's jaws and across the waters and on out of the mist, and over the sea it flew through the air as if it were a bird, not a ship, and at last landed with a great splash, miles and miles and miles away from the Dragon of the North Sea.

Erik's men cheered and threw their helmets in the air, and Ragnar Forkbeard climbed down, and after that no one ever dared to say he had ever lost either his courage, his voice or his wits ever again.

THE OLD MAN OF THE SEA

AFTER THEIR ENCOUNTER with the Sea Dragon, Erik and his men looked at their ship, Golden Dragon, and saw that the monster had done much damage and that water was flooding in at the stern.

'We must bail this water out,' said Erik, 'or we shall not keep afloat for long.'

'But how can we bail?' cried his men. 'We have not one single bucket between us. We are lost for sure!'

'Then we must use our helmets,' said Erik, and he got down with his men and started to bail the water out of Golden Dragon with his own helmet.

But the more they bailed the water out, the more the water seemed to flood in.

'We shall sink before nightfall,' whispered Erik's men one to the other.

'Unless we reach land, we are dead men,' they said.

Thorkhild stood by the great oar at the back of the ship and steered. 'But I do not know where we are,' he said to himself, 'nor have I any idea in which direction there is land. I fear we are lost for sure.'

Just then Thorkhild saw a shape in the water, which looked as if it were following the boat. Thorkhild watched and watched this shape and it seemed to him that it was an old man swimming all alone in the sea.

'Hey there!' called out Thorkhild. 'Who are you? Swimming alone in the icy waves so far from land?'

The old man looked up out of the water at Thorkhild and laughed. But he said not a word.

'How do you come to swim so fast?' asked Thorkhild.

Again the old man in the water looked up and laughed. But again he said not a word.

'Can you help us find land?' asked Thorkhild, 'For we are badly damaged and will sink before nightfall.'

At this the old man did not laugh. He looked up at Thorkhild and said, 'I'll show you land, but if I do, one of you must come and join me in the icy waves.'

Thorkhild felt a sudden cold to the marrow of his bones, for he knew then that this was the Old Man of the Sea and that to join him in the icy waves meant certain death. But he said to the Old Man of the Sea, 'Show us where we can find land.'

The Old Man of the Sea laughed and replied, 'But which one of you will come and join me in the icy waves?'

'Show us land and I shall come and join you in the icy waves.'

When Thorkhild had said the words, the Old Man of the Sea laughed again and took the great oar in his hands and turned it until Golden Dragon was heading due North. But Thorkhild grieved in his mind, for he knew that the Old Man of the Sea always took a life before ever he saved one.

'I am as good as dead,' he said to himself, 'but at least my comrades will reach land.' But still he grieved in his mind, because he knew that the Old Man of the Sea was full of tricks, and no one could ever put his trust in him.

Well, they sailed on like this for many hours, and every other hour Erik would look up from his bailing and say to Thorkhild, 'Any sign of land?'

And Thorkhild would reply, 'We are heading straight for it.' And Erik would nod and encourage his men, and they would all bail faster as the water kept flooding in.

At length, Thorkhild leaned over the side again and shouted down to the Old Man of the Sea, 'How much further?'

And the Old Man of the Sea laughed loud and long, and said, 'Far enough for you!' And Thorkhild looked towards the horizon and saw an island. 'Land ahead!' cried Thorkhild, and Erik and his men stood up and gave a mighty cheer.

'We are saved!' said Erik. 'Tonight we shall celebrate and dry ourselves around a great fire! And we shall drink a toast to Thorkhild, who steered us safe to dry land.'

And all his men gave another mighty cheer, but Thorkhild looked grave and said, 'I shall not be with you.' Then he explained to Erik how the Old Man of the Sea had guided the boat to land, and that in return one of their number must go and join him in the icy waves. 'And since I made the bargain with the Old Man of the Sea,' said Thorkhild, 'it is right that I go and join him in the icy waves.'

Just then they all heard the sound of laughter and they looked over the side and saw the Old Man of the Sea grinning up at them.

'Well,' he said, 'I am waiting for you.'

'You need wait no longer,' said Thorkhild and he got up to go.

But Erik's men said to Thorkhild, 'Don't go! It will be death to join him in the icy waves, and we are almost at land!'

But Thorkhild replied, 'No! The Old Man of the Sea has kept his side of the bargain. I must now keep mine,' and he stood up on the side of Golden Dragon about to throw himself into the icy waves.

Then Erik took Thorkhild's arm and said, 'The Old Man of the Sea is full of tricks. Wait until we see this island he has brought us to, and then you may go and join him in the icy waves.'

At which words Thorkhild nodded and stepped back into the boat.

'I am waiting for you,' cried the Old Man of the Sea, 'or aren't you going to keep your side of the bargain?' And his eyes glinted wickeder and trickier than ever.

'Have no fear,' replied Thorkhild. 'I shall keep my side of the bargain, for you have kept yours.'

'Then come and join me in the icy waves!' grinned the Old Man of the Sea.

'First may I fetch some bacon so that we may eat together?' asked Thorkhild.

'Very well,' said the Old Man of the Sea, and he waited while Thorkhild took down a large flitch of bacon that hung from the mast, and tied it round his waist. At this the Old Man of the Sea laughed a loud laugh, then he said, 'I am waiting for you. Now come and join me in the icy waves.'

'First may I sharpen my knife so I may cut the bacon?' asked Thorkhild.

'Very well,' said the Old Man of the Sea, and he waited while Thorkhild took a whetstone from under his seat and began to sharpen his knife until it shone. Then the Old Man of the Sea laughed twice as loud and long, and said, 'Well! I am waiting for you … now come and join me in the icy waves.'

'One last thing,' said Thorkhild.

'What is it?' cried the Old Man of the Sea.

'I need some rope,' said Thorkhild, 'to hang my bacon up in your kitchen in the icy waves.'

Well, at this the Old Man of the Sea laughed three times as loud and long and said: 'Very well!' So Thorkhild tied a length of rope around his waist and said, 'Now I am quite ready to join you in the icy waves.' And he climbed onto the side of Golden Dragon and prepared to jump.

But just then one of Erik's men shouted out, 'It's a trick!' and he pointed to the island which they had reached by now, and they all saw that it wasn't an island at all but a gigantic narwhal, four times as long as Golden Dragon and four times as high as her mainmast.

'Old Man of the Sea!' called out Thorkhild, 'you didn't keep your side of the bargain, but I shall keep mine!' And before anyone could stop him, he had leapt off the side of Golden Dragon and had joined the Old Man of the Sea in the icy waves.

'Thorkhild!' cried Erik, 'the sea is too cold, and the Old Man of the Sea is too tricky – you will die for sure!'

But while they had been talking, Thorkhild had taken the flitch of bacon and rubbed its grease all over himself so that the icy waters ran off his skin like water off a duck's back. And when he reached the Old Man of the Sea he grabbed him round his skinny neck,

and took his newly sharpened knife and cut off his beard with one slice! Then he pulled on the rope, which he had round his waist, and, because he'd fixed the other end to the mast, he was able to pull himself back on board before the Old Man of the Sea could drag him back under!

Then Thorkhild nailed the Old Man of the Sea's beard to the mainmast and they all laughed and pointed at it. And the Old Man of the Sea was so furious and so ashamed that he swam off without another word, and the gigantic narwhal followed after him.

When the great creature had gone, Erik and his men saw on the distant horizon a tiny speck of land. Night had fallen by the time they reached it, but they rowed ashore and lit a fire on the beach. And many was the toast they drank that night to Thorkhild, who had not only steered them safe to land but had become the first person ever to out-trick the Old Man of the Sea!

HOW ERIK AND HIS MEN WERE TURNED TO STONE

AFTER THEY HAD CELEBRATED their safe arrival on shore, Erik and his men slept soundly through the night. The next day, they were up at first light, eager to see what sort of a land they had arrived in.

But their hearts sank as they looked around. There was not a tree nor a bush nor a blade of grass to be seen. Neither were there any signs of animals or even any birds, only rocks and stones and ice.

'We have found a land that has been forgotten by Life itself,' said Erik.

And his men said, 'Without trees we have no wood to repair Golden Dragon, and without plants or animals or birds we shall starve to death here on this lonely shore.'

But Erik said, 'Let us not waste our breath talking.'

So they hauled Golden Dragon onto the beach, and then they built a shelter of stones. That night, Ragnar Forkbeard said to Erik: 'This is a strange country that is shunned by all living things.'

Erik replied, 'We must not stay here long.'

But when he looked at the great hole in the side of their ship, Golden Dragon, he shook his head and said, 'We shall need the wood from many trees to put our ship to rights. And I fear we shall all be dead before any trees grow in this land.'

Erik did not sleep that night. He sat up gazing into the darkness. He had never seen a night so black, nor heard a night so silent in all his life. But then, just before dawn had begun to break, he saw a light in the far, far distance.

He wrapped his cloak around himself and stepped out over the rocky shore. As he walked towards the light, dawn began to break, and as the sun rose the light grew dimmer until it was lost altogether, and all he could see were rocks and boulders, the one indistinguishable from the other. So he returned back to his men and did not mention what he had seen.

HOW ERIK AND HIS MEN WERE TURNED TO STONE

The next night Erik again sat and watched, and again, just before dawn, he saw the light. This time he jumped up at once and ran as fast as he could towards it, but again the sun rose before he could reach it, and he returned none the wiser.

On the third night, when all his men were fast asleep, Erik took a blazing torch and stumbled along the rocky shore towards the point where he had seen the light. Sure enough, just before dawn, he saw it for the third time, only now he was much much closer, and he could see there was not one light but six lights. Before dawn had risen he reached the spot where the lights were, and there he saw the strangest sight. He saw three black cats sitting on a rock washing themselves, and their eyes shone like bright torches and lit up whatever they looked at.

Erik watched the three strange creatures as the sun rose, and as it rose the three cats washed themselves slower and slower, and they grew greyer and greyer, and their eyes shone less and less, until, by the time the sun had risen above the horizon, all three had turned to solid stone.

Erik went over to them, but now they were not the shape of cats any more but just three grey rocks.

Erik shook his head and said, 'This place is enchanted for sure. We must leave at once.'

Then he retraced his steps towards where his ship, Golden Dragon, lay on her side on the shore. But he walked and walked, and still he could see no sign of her. At length he reached the spot where his men had built their shelter of stones, and there it was … but of his men there was no sign.

Erik sat and gazed for a long time at the sea washing against the great grey rock that lay on the beach. And then suddenly he leapt to his feet, crying, 'That great grey rock wasn't there last night!' And he strode over to it and gazed up at its height, and its height was exactly the height of Golden Dragon. Then he paced out its length from one end to the other, and its length was exactly the length of Golden Dragon…

'I am too late!' he cried. 'My ship has been turned to grey rock!'

Then he turned to the shelter of stones that he and his men had built, and he noticed for the first time the grey rocks strewn about inside and the grey rocks scattered over the beach, and Erik put his head in his hands and sat down in despair saying, 'Is it possible? Can it be that even my men have been turned to stones and rocks? Ragnar Forkbeard and Thorkhild and even Sven the Strong? Who could have done this? Who has laid this enchantment upon this whole land?'

And the wind blew and the salt spray of the sea mixed with the salt of his tears, and Erik was more alone at that moment than at any other moment in his life.

That night he hid himself near the rock where he had seen the three black cats with shining eyes. Sure enough, some time before dawn he heard a noise. It was someone or something approaching in the pitch black night. Erik could see nothing, but he heard the click-clack of hooves stepping over the rocks and the tapping of a stick.

Then he heard a strange voice saying, 'There ... where are you my lovelies?'

Erik waited a bit and pretty soon he heard another sound – like a deep rumble. At first Erik was frightened, but then he realised it was just a cat purring. And he saw two lights begin to glow as gradually one of the rocks turned back into a cat with shining eyes. Then by the light of its shining eyes he saw the Enchanter who had laid the spell on the island. He was an old man dressed in black, and under his robe instead of feet he had hooves. The black cat turned and looked up at its master, and its eyes shone on his face, and Erik could see that instead of eyes the old Enchanter had two grey stones.

HOW ERIK AND HIS MEN WERE TURNED TO STONE

'Where's my other beauty?' muttered the Enchanter, and he reached out a blind hand and groped until he felt the second rock. Then he started stroking the rock, until it seemed to shiver a little, and then it began to shake, and Erik heard the cat's purring again as the rock changed gradually into the second cat with shining eyes. Then the blind old Enchanter reached out and stroked the third grey rock so that it too trembled and came back to life.

'Come, my beauties,' said the Enchanter, 'light my way.'

Erik watched as the three cats stretched and yawned and then rose from their rock and led the way down into a deep chasm. And their eyes lit up the grey rocks on every side, and the blind old Enchanter walked behind them just as if he could see.

When they got to the bottom of the chasm, the old man pushed at a great rock which slid aside to reveal a cave, then he stood at the mouth of the cave and called out, 'Daughter! Daughter!'

A thin girl, white as paper, came out into the light from the cats' eyes and stood there blinking.

'Father,' she said, 'when may I be free?'

'Soon enough, Freya,' said the Enchanter, 'when I have made this island beautiful enough for you.'

'But even to see the sun would be beauty enough for me,' said the girl.

'What good is the sunlight if it has nothing to shine on?' replied the old man. 'Stay where you are, daughter, for bit by bit I am making this island green and pleasant.'

When Erik heard all this, he leapt up from behind the rock with his sword in his hand and cried out: 'You are blind! Can't you see you've turned it to nothing but rocks and stones?'

As soon as he spoke, they all turned to look at him, and the cats' eyes shone straight at him, lighting him up, and as they did so he felt his blood freezing, and he knew that he too was turning to stone.

But at that moment, Freya, the Enchanter's daughter ran up to him and cried: 'Don't be afraid! They dare not shine their eyes on me,' and as she spoke the three cats turned their heads away as one. But when Erik tried to move he knew he was already half stone. Then he spoke very slowly, and said to Freya, 'My ... sword ...'

He could say no more, but at once Freya took his sword from his hand and cut off the heads of those three creatures, and the moment she did so they changed from cats into demons that flew away and were gone forever.

HOW ERIK AND HIS MEN WERE TURNED TO STONE

And at that moment the sun began to rise.

'What is happening?' cried the blind old Enchanter.

'Follow me,' said Erik, and slowly, very slowly, he led the way back out of the chasm, past the rock where he had first seen the three cats, and back along the shoreline. And Freya and the old Enchanter followed.

By the time they reached the shelter of stones, the sun had fully risen. Then Erik slowly turned to the blind old Enchanter, and slowly, because he was still half stone he reached his hand towards the stones that were his eyes, and plucked them out.

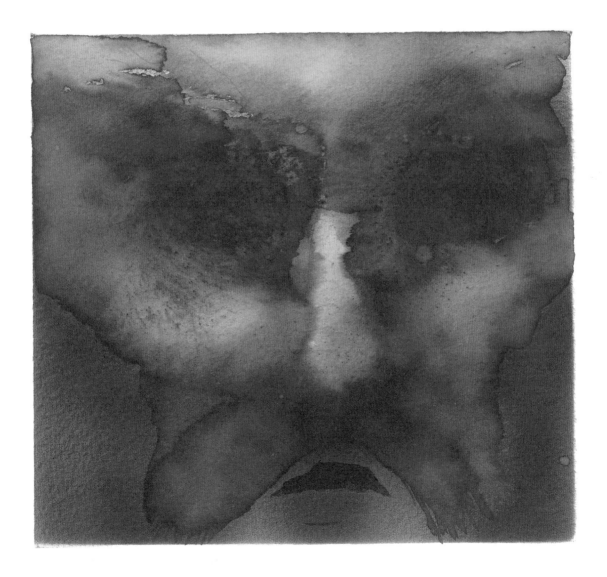

HOW ERIK AND HIS MEN WERE TURNED TO STONE

And then the Enchanter was blind no more and he saw what he had done. He saw the rocks that were Erik's men, and he saw the great grey rock that had been their ship, Golden Dragon, and he saw the desolate island of stones and rocks and ice, and he wept.

And the moment his first tear touched the earth, a most wonderful and amazing thing happened. The enchantment began to lift and the grey rocks on the beach moved and shook and then stood up and were Erik's men again. And so too every rock and stone and pebble along that shoreline began to turn and tremble, and turn back into a living thing. Some into flowers and plants, some into animals and birds, until the whole coast was green and teeming with life again. And there on the shore were Thorkhild and Sven the Strong and Ragnar Forkbeard. And there too lay Golden Dragon herself.

The old Enchanter begged his daughter's forgiveness that in his blindness he had imprisoned her and allowed the island to be turned to desolation by the three cat-demons.

Freya gave him her hand and at once the great mountain behind them turned back into a palace, and there Erik and his men lived well and happily all the time they took to repair their ship, Golden Dragon.

ERIK AT THE ENCHANTER'S COURT

WHILE ERIK AND HIS MEN were staying at the court of the old Enchanter and his daughter, Freya, a strange adventure happened.

One day the Enchanter said he must go away for several days, and that he must leave his daughter, Freya, in their care.

'Have no fear,' said Erik, 'I shall look after her as if she were my own dear child.' And so the Enchanter left, riding on a huge black pig, and Erik and his men continued to repair their ship, Golden Dragon.

That night, when the wind was howling outside round the palace and they were all gathered in the great hall around a blazing fire, the Enchanter's daughter, Freya, stood up and said, 'Which one of you has taken my shoes?'

Erik and his men looked one to the other, and they all shook their heads and said not one of them would have ever dreamt of taking Freya's shoes.

'They were on my feet but a moment ago,' said the Enchanter's daughter, 'and now they are gone,' and she showed her bare feet to everyone. And Erik's men all agreed that they were elegant white feet, but no one had any idea of what had happened to her shoes.

So they ate some more and passed the mead jug round, and by and by Freya rose to her feet once more, and her face was clouded.

'What is the trouble, Freya?' asked Erik.

And Freya said, 'It grieves me to ask … but which of you has taken my ring?'

Well, Erik's men looked one to the other, and then they shook their heads, and Erik replied, 'Freya, we are not thieves and robbers … not one of us would ever take your ring.'

'It was here on my finger but a moment ago,' said the Enchanter's daughter, 'and now it is gone,' and she showed them her hand. Erik's men all agreed it was a delicate white hand, but none of them had any idea of what had happened to her ring.

So they ate some more and passed the mead jug round, and the fire burned brighter and redder. Then all of a sudden they heard a cry, and Erik and his men turned, and there was Freya, the Enchanter's daughter, standing as naked as the day that she was born.

'Who has taken my clothes?' she cried, and she burst into tears.

And Erik and his men looked from one to the other in amazement, for only the moment before she had been sitting there in her slender white robe. Erik took off his cloak and put it over her shoulders, and put his arm around her and said, 'Who could have done this?'

And Ragnar Forkbeard stood up and replied, 'There is no one here who would do such a thing. We are all sworn to protect this girl.'

But Freya frowned and said, 'If the thief is not found before my father returns, he will banish you from this island, whether your ship is finished or no.' And with that she ran to her room.

Then Erik said to his men, 'No one has been in nor out of this Great Hall in this time. The thief must still be here.' So they began to search the Great Hall. They searched under every seat and every table and every bed in the Great Hall. But they could not find the thief. Erik said to his men, 'We must not sleep until this thief is found.'

So they started to search the whole palace. They searched the corridors, the bedrooms, the rooms of state, the kitchens, the cellars, the turret rooms, and the closets, the cupboards and the chimneys, under the floor boards and behind the tapestries. They even looked for secret passages and hidden rooms and found plenty. They even searched the old Enchanter's private study but they could find neither hide nor hair of any thief, nor any shred of Freya's clothes.

Dawn was breaking, and Erik and his men were very tired for they had been searching hard all night, when Freya appeared before them and said, 'Well, have you found this thief?'

They all shook their heads, and Freya looked at them and said, 'The shoes and the robe were presents my father gave me before he left. If the thief is not found, I fear my father will turn you back to stones in his anger!'

So Erik and his men redoubled their efforts. All day they searched the palace grounds. They looked in every conceivable place: in the stables and the out-houses, in the barns and chicken houses and the wash house and the cattle sheds, under hedges and in ditches, in the grass and amongst the flowers, up trees and in the bushes. They looked everywhere.

And that evening they all assembled together and Freya asked them, 'Well? Have you found the thief?'

They all shook their heads, and Freya frowned and said, 'The ring was my grandmother's ring. My father gave it to me before he left. If the thief is not found before he returns, I fear he will go mad with anger and shut me away again in that dark cave.'

Then Erik stood up and said, 'That we will never allow him to do! We shall find this thief before your father returns.' And with that they started to search the whole island. They searched the valleys and the mountains, the beaches and fields, the caves and woods and even the rivers and rocky ravines and the dark, deep forests. And all the while their ship, Golden Dragon, lay on her side on the beach, and not a nail was nailed in her nor a plank was sawn, and the hole in her stern was as big as ever.

On the day when the old Enchanter was to return, Erik and his men gathered in the Great Hall, and they each looked anxiously at the others. Then Freya appeared before them and said, 'Surely you have found the thief now?'

But Erik shook his head, 'We have searched every stone and every leaf of this island, but we have found neither hair nor hide of this thief.'

Just then the door burst open and in strode the old Enchanter himself.

Erik and his men threw themselves on their knees before him, and Erik explained what had happened.

'But please don't turn these men to stone,' cried Freya, 'for they have searched night and day for the thief.'

'And please don't shut your daughter back in the cave,' said Erik, 'for we shall carry on searching until we find the thief!' And they all looked at the old Enchanter.

And to their surprise he did not go mad with anger. He did not banish his daughter to the cave, nor turn Erik and his men to stone, nor even banish them from the island whether their boat was finished or no. Instead he smiled.

'You need look no further for the thief,' he said, 'for he is here in this room.'

Erik's men looked at each other, and Freya looked from her father to Erik to Thorkhild and Sven the Strong and from Sven the Strong to Ragnar Forkbeard and then back to her father.

'But we have searched every nook and cranny of this Great Hall,' said Erik. 'The thief could not possibly be here.'

'There is one place you have not looked,' said the old Enchanter, and he called his daughter over to him and sat her on his knee. 'You never looked here!' With that he quickly put his hand into Freya's hair and pulled out a little goblin as black as soot, which kicked and screamed in a little high voice, 'Let me go!' But the old Enchanter held it firm between his fingers.

'This is the mischief-maker,' said the old Enchanter. 'This flibbertigibbet! This snatch-troll! I thought it was harmless, but as soon as my back was turned it got up to its old tricks, eh? Very well …'

And he put a spell on the little creature and it turned into a little black puppy, which he gave to his daughter, saying, 'There! Now it may get into mischief, but it won't stop these men doing their work in future.'

Then the old Enchanter declared a feast that night, and the next day, Erik and his men got back to repairing their ship.

ERIK AND THE DOGFIGHTERS

WHILE ERIK AND HIS MEN were staying at the palace of the old Enchanter and his daughter, an even stranger adventure happened.

One morning they were hard at work on their ship, Golden Dragon, having almost finished repairing the great hole in the stern that the Sea Dragon had made, when they saw another ship far out to sea.

Erik strained his eyes and then said, 'I have never seen a ship like that before.'

Ragnar Forkbeard too peered into the distance and then said, 'This is the strangest ship I ever saw!'

Thorkhild raised his hand to his eyes and said, 'It has six sails and each sail is round like the sun. And how tall the masts are!'

The old Enchanter came to the shore, and when he saw the ship approaching he shook his head, and sighed a deep sigh. 'I fear your work on Golden Dragon has been in vain. None of us shall live to see another sunrise.'

Erik put his hand to his sword and so too did each of his men.

'Farewell, daughter,' said the old Enchanter. 'Even I am not powerful enough to save you from this evil that now approaches.' And tears came to the old man's eyes.

But Erik gripped his arm and said, 'What is this strange ship that approaches? What foe does it bring that strikes such terror into your heart?'

The old Enchanter gazed at him and said, 'I know this ship from the fearful past. I have seen it once before from another land. It brings death and destruction for it brings the Dogfighters to our peaceful shore.'

Erik and his men looked out at the ship that was fast approaching, and they could see dark figures lining the deck and the glint of many swords.

'Whoever it brings,' said Erik, 'we shall defend this island to the last breath in our bodies.'

But the old man shook his head. 'How can you succeed where all have failed before?' And all the time the Dogfighters' ship drew nearer and nearer.

'Take your daughter to the great cave in the mountain, and we shall find you when the fight is done,' said Erik.

But the old Enchanter shook his head. 'You cannot fight the Dogfighters. Come with us, and perhaps we shall escape somehow …'

But Erik replied, 'We shall never leave our ship, Golden Dragon, for it is certain such an enemy would steal or destroy it.' And all the time the Dogfighters' ship drew nearer and nearer, and now the men on the shore could see the glint of steel helmets in the wintry northern sun.

'Come away, quickly, while there is still time!' cried the old Enchanter, but Erik and his men had drawn their swords and already they were taking up their battle stations.

The old Enchanter shook his head and turned to go, but Freya, his daughter, stood where she was and said, 'Father, I will stay with these brave men and face this enemy. For I would rather die here and now on this shore than live in fear and shadow in the cave in the mountain.'

The old man tried to speak, but no words came to his lips. He held his daughter to him, and then they both hid behind some rocks, as the Dogfighters' ship drew closer to the shore.

Erik and his men peered hard to make out their enemy, and now they could see that each of them did indeed wear a steel helmet and each helmet was shaped like a great dog's head!

'Are these men with the heads of dogs?' said Erik. 'Or dogs with the bodies of men?' And secretly each of his companions felt sick with fear.

Ragnar Forkbeard turned to Erik and said, 'How can we fight such creatures as these?' And Erik stared at the grey sea and said, 'Even I fear it is hopeless.'

And they watched as the dog-headed warriors began to leap out of their strange craft. Then Sven the Strong took Erik to one side and whispered to him, 'Erik! Never have I felt such fear as I feel now.' And Erik looked into his eyes, and saw the fear there, and said, 'Then it is indeed hopeless.' And Erik threw his sword onto the stony beach and looked at his men, and they each one of them saw the fear in his eyes.

As the Dogfighters waded nearer, the companions saw that, though the waves were high, the dog-headed warriors stood three feet above the highest!

Then Ragnar Forkbeard also threw his sword onto the stony beach and said, 'If Erik cannot fight these creatures, how can we? I too have never felt such fear.' Then the shore rang to the clatter of swords as each of Erik's men threw his sword down onto the stony beach … all except for Sven the Strong, and he said, 'What has happened to us? Many times in my life I have been afraid, yet it has not made me throw down my sword …'

And Erik and his men looked up and saw the dog-headed warriors wading through the boiling waters nearer and nearer to the shore and their eyes glittered in their helmets cold and hard. And then even Sven the Strong threw down his sword onto the stony beach, saying, '… and yet, I know, even I cannot fight with such fear in my heart …'

But just then they heard another voice behind them, saying, 'It is not fear that you feel!' And they turned, and there was the old Enchanter's daughter standing white and frail in the wintry northern sun, but her face was strong.

'I feel fear,' said Erik to Freya, 'because I know that no one has ever faced these Dogfighters and lived …' and he sank to his knees as if a great weight were pressing down on him, and all the time the dog-headed warriors waded closer and closer.

'But you are wrong!' cried Freya. 'Don't you remember there is one here who has faced them and lived!'

At this Sven the Strong looked up, and Thorkhild looked up, and they said, 'Who? Which one of us has ever faced these fearful creatures?' And Freya replied, 'None of you have, but my father has!' And without another word Sven the Strong strode over to the old man and said, 'Of course … If you know them from the fearful past as you say, you have met with them and lived. Tell us how!'

And the old Enchanter wept, 'It is hopeless.'

'Tell us what happened!' cried Sven the Strong, and he lifted the old man up in his hands as the Dogfighters reached the beach at last.

The old man looked into Sven's eyes, 'Did I escape?' he asked.

'Of course you did!' cried Sven the Strong and he saw the fear flicker a moment in the old Enchanter's eyes.

41

'But they are here! The Dogfighters are upon us!' cried the old man. But Sven did not turn round. He did not see the first Dogfighter reach the first of Erik's men …

'But this is the second time!' cried Sven. 'You escaped before! How? How?'

'How?' cried the old man, and he shut his eyes.

'It was not fear you felt,' cried his daughter. 'Don't you remember telling me – it was not fear you felt …'

'No …' said the old man, and the first of the Dogfighters struck the first of Erik's men to the white bone … there, where he knelt on the stony beach.

'It was not fear …' said the old Enchanter, 'I remember now! It was the fear of fear … It was a spell the Dogfighters cast, for they themselves are cold cowards.' And the old Enchanter opened his eyes, raised his arms, and for an instant the wintry northern sun turned black – no more than the blinking of an eye – and then Sven the Strong gave a great cry: 'Erik! It is a trick! These Dogfighters would make us afraid of being afraid! We are often frightened, but we are not cowards!'

And before the words had left his lips, Erik's sword was back in his hand, 'I am not afraid of fear,' he cried. 'Fear is like an old friend, who shouts by my side,' and he raised his sword and struck the Dogfighter a mighty blow across the shoulders, and the steel helmet rang, and before the echo had died amongst the grey rocks every one of Erik's men – Thorkhild and Ragnar Forkbeard and Sven the Strong and the rest – had taken up their swords off the stony beach. The battle against the Dogfighters had begun …

THORKHILD AND THE STARSWORD

ERIK AND HIS MEN fought the Dogfighters hand to hand and sword to sword. And each of the Dogfighters stood head and shoulders three feet above each of Erik's men. And their swords were twice as long and twice as broad as the swords that Erik and his men had in their hands. 'How can we fight against such fearful odds?' thought each and every one of Erik's men. But they said not a word. They stood their ground and blow for blow, thrust for thrust they fought the Dogfighters … on that stony beach … beneath the wintry northern sun.

Ragnar Forkbeard was cut through the arm and fell down on the stony beach, but, before his dog-headed foe could raise its sword again, Sven the Strong had run his sword through the creature's heart, and it gave a cry like a hound of hell, and turned and stumbled back into foaming sea, and the white foam turned red. Then Erik looked up and saw another wave of Dogfighters leap out from their boat and wade across the churning waters.

'There are too many for us!' he cried to Thorkhild.

'Too many or too few – what choice have we?' shouted Thorkhild, and he dived to miss the swinging blade of the biggest of the Dogfighters – he whose helmet was made of gold that shone so bright it reflected the flashing of a hundred swords. Then Thorkhild grabbed the creature by the foot, and pulled with all his might so that it toppled from the jagged rock into the boiling waves. And Thorkhild caught its mighty sword as it flew from its hand and with one blow he severed the creature's head in its golden helmet. The head roared for a moment, and then it roared without sound, and then it rolled beneath the waves, and Thorkhild turned with his new sword held high above him.

At this moment Erik heard a strange noise. It was like a groan from hell, and he looked and saw the Dogfighters stopped, still, staring at the sword that Thorkhild held. Whereupon Erik's men seized their chance and cleaved those terrible creatures through to their backbones, each and every one of them, so that before they had turned to fight again they were already dead upon the stony beach … all but one.

And that staggered towards Thorkhild, still gazing at the sword, the bright blood oozing from beneath its helmet, and it stretched out its hand towards the great sword, and they heard it say one word: 'Starsword!' before it too fell onto the stony beach.

Then Thorkhild moved forward, still holding the sword above his head, and the second wave of Dogfighters had frozen in their tracks and stood there motionless in the rolling sea, with the waters breaking about them, staring at the sword. But as Thorkhild stepped into the waves himself, they turned and surged back through the waters to their ship.

And at this a great cheer went up from Erik's men, there where they stood. But Erik did not cheer. He gripped his sword and cried out, 'We must stop them going back to whatever hellish land they came from, lest they return here with more of their kind!'

But Erik's men looked at each other, and murmured, 'We could never fight them in those icy waters!'

And Erik, seeing his men hesitate, turned to them and said, 'You think we have won a great victory? But what when we are gone? Who then shall prevent these hounds of hell from returning to take revenge on the old Enchanter, and his daughter?'

'But the sea is deep!' cried his men. 'The waves are cold … Our swords would be frozen in our hands.'

'Where is your courage?' cried Erik.

But then the old Enchanter stepped forward and said, 'They are right! How could you fight these creatures amidst the icy waves? And see! They have already reached their ship. Best let them go!'

'I have sworn to protect your daughter,' replied Erik. 'Our victory just now was but to protect ourselves. Unless I prevent these creatures going, I shall have broken my vow.'

Then Sven the Strong stepped forward: 'I will come with you, Erik,' he said. 'Though no one else goes with us, you shall have my sword beside you.'

And then Ragnar Forkbeard rose up on his good arm and said, 'I too will come,' and he struggled to his feet, with his arm's blood still streaming onto the rock. Then Erik's men hung their heads. They were put to shame by their wounded comrade, and one by one they stepped forward to join in the desperate venture.

'You will all die!' called Freya, the old Enchanter's daughter.

'Do not go after them!' cried the old Enchanter. But Erik and his men moved down to the water's edge.

'Stay where you are!' said a third voice. And they all turned to see Thorkhild standing where he was, the Starsword still held above his head.

'Here is a power I have never felt before,' he was saying, and the Starsword seemed to be trembling in his hands. 'This sword is alive. I can feel it! I can feel it turning in my hands!'

And as they watched in wonder – Erik and his men, Freya and the old Enchanter – they saw the strangest sight. The Starsword seemed to glow, bright as the brightest stars, as Thorkhild held it there above him. And then slowly it seemed to rise into the air, leaving his grasp, and there it hung above him. Then the Starsword turned and began to fly over the foam-flecked waves. Sure and steady it flew. It flew towards the ship that now was speeding the Dogfighters away, inch by inch, drawing closer and closer over the toiling sea. And the Dogfighters rowed, fast and furious, to find the offshore breeze. But the sword drew closer and closer, glowing brighter now in the wintry northern sky.

'Who has ever seen such a sword as this?' said Erik, as they gazed from the shore and saw the strange ship with the round sails catch the wind and start to run before it. But the Starsword seemed to catch the wind too, and before the ship reached the horizon, Erik and his men saw the mighty sword strike it. It cut through the very timbers, as if they were snow, and it seemed as if the very entrails of the boat were poured out into the ocean, and the icy water flooded in, and the Dogfighters' ship began to sink beneath the waves.

And then the sound reached the shore, faint and far-off – like the braying and barking of all the hounds of darkness – before the Dogfighters too were gone, lost beneath the pitiless ocean, and nothing remained.

Then Erik and his men gave a mighty cheer, and they lifted Thorkhild up on their shoulders and carried him back to the Enchanter's palace. And they held a great celebration that night, and everyone rejoiced at the great victory.

Only Thorkhild was silent. He neither smiled nor joined in the feasting. So Erik took his seat beside him at the table and said, 'What is the matter, Thorkhild? Today you have saved us all from the most dangerous of foes and you have made this island safe for the old Enchanter and his daughter. You should be happy, and yet you seem sad.'

Thorkhild looked at Erik and said, 'Today, for a brief moment, I possessed the greatest sword I have ever seen or held in my hands. Now it is gone, and I fear I shall never see nor hold in my hands such a sword again.'

And no matter what Erik, or his men, or the old Enchanter or even his daughter could say or do, Thorkhild would not join in the celebrations. Instead he left the palace, and went and sat on the stony shore in the darkness – gazing out to sea, where he had last seen the Starsword, grieving that he would never hold it in his hands again.

THE THREE
WONDERFUL GIFTS

SOME TIME AFTER THE BATTLE with the Dogfighters, Erik came to the old Enchanter and said, 'Our ship, Golden Dragon, is now ready. We must leave you before the snows come.'

Then they shook hands and the old Enchanter gave Erik and his companions three boxes. 'Inside each is a precious gift,' said the old Enchanter. 'The first is for today. The second is for tomorrow. And the third is for yesterday. But do not open them until you truly have need of them.'

Erik wondered to himself what such gifts could be, but he thanked the old man. And then Freya, the Enchanter's daughter, gave Erik a cloak, saying, 'No matter what the wind nor the snow may do, this will always keep you warm.'

Erik took the gifts and put them in a secret cupboard aboard Golden Dragon. Then they carried Ragnar Forkbeard aboard who, alone, lay still sick from his wound. And thus they left the island of the old Enchanter.

Many days passed without sight of land, and the ship became their home, and they slept on the rolling seas with the stars above. But one night the stars were no longer there, and the next day the skies were dark with storm clouds.

'I fear the snows will soon be upon us,' said Erik. 'We must find land or we shall be lost for sure.'

But even as he spoke, a single snowflake floated down out of the heavy sky and landed on the deck of Golden Dragon. At that moment, however, they heard a cry and they looked to the horizon, and there was a speck of land. So they set their sails and were soon speeding towards it. But even as they did so, two snowflakes floated down out of the heavy sky and landed on the deck of Golden Dragon.

'We must be swift,' said Erik as they reached the shore, and he ordered all the food and all the clothing that they had to be carried ashore, so they might make their camp there.

But even as they began to move all the food and the clothing the snow began to fall … thick and fast it fell out of the silent sky onto the roaring sea.

Soon his men had disappeared from view and the snow blotted out the very land itself, and only Erik and Ragnar Forkbeard remained on board Golden Dragon.

Then the sea began to swell, and the wind whipped up the waves until they lashed across the deck of Golden Dragon, and Ragnar Forkbeard said, 'I pray we see our comrades again.' But, even as he spoke, the waves grew higher, and the ship pitched and rolled like a wild horse, and the snow swirled, and the wind roared.

'I will cast another anchor!' said Erik, 'for I fear one will not hold us in such a storm.'

But even as he spoke the waves grew higher, and the ship tossed and reared and rocked, and strained at the anchor, and the timbers creaked.

Then suddenly it all went still, and Erik looked at Ragnar Forkbeard and said, 'Perhaps the storm is over.'

THE THREE WONDERFUL GIFTS

Ragnar Forkbeard shook his head, but before even he could speak there was a terrible noise. The snow flew up. The wind bellowed, and a wave six times as high as the mainmast crashed over Golden Dragon and sent her spinning and twisting through the blasting waters that tore at her decks like a giant's hands, snapping the timbers and snatching at the two men who lay on board.

Erik and Ragnar Forkbeard clung on as best they could, but they knew their anchor had gone, and they were now the ocean's toy as they whirled away into the depths of the storm and the gathering night.

All that night they tossed and span in that terrible tempest, until their heads were dizzy and their bodies ached, but the wonder of it was that, when dawn broke, the storm had vanished, and Golden Dragon was riding as if at anchor in a little bay.

'How shall we regain our companions?' said Erik to Ragnar Forkbeard. 'I dare not risk taking Golden Dragon single-handed out of this little bay into the open sea.'

'Then we must wait for them to find us,' answered Ragnar Forkbeard.

'But we shall be dead before ever they do,' Erik replied, 'from cold and hunger.'

'Have we no food?' asked Ragnar Forkbeard.

'None,' replied Erik. 'That was all taken off the ship and carried ashore.'

'Have we no clothing?' asked Ragnar Forkbeard.

'None,' replied Erik. 'That too was all taken off the ship and carried ashore.'

'Then indeed we shall die of cold and hunger,' said Ragnar Forkbeard, 'before ever we are found.'

And Erik the Viking, and Ragnar Forkbeard gazed across to the white hills, and were silent.

Finally Ragnar Forkbeard spoke. 'I will not lie here,' he said, 'for death to find me helpless and without hope. Let us leave Golden Dragon, and seek our companions on foot.'

'But they may be far,' said Erik.

'They may be near,' said Ragnar Forkbeard.

'But the way will all be snow and ice,' said Erik. 'If we do not find them by nightfall, I am afraid we shall die.'

'Let us try,' said Ragnar Forkbeard.

'You are not strong enough for such a journey,' said Erik.

THE THREE WONDERFUL GIFTS

But Ragnar Forkbeard had risen to his feet. 'I must be,' he said, and turned to go. At that moment Erik gave a great shout, so that Ragnar Forkbeard looked round in surprise.

'Of course!' cried Erik. 'Can it be that the storm has driven our wits from us? We may have no food. We may have no clothes, but we have the old Enchanter's gifts, and now, if at anytime, we truly have need of them!'

And without another word he opened up the secret cupboard where he had hidden them.

'This is the gift for today,' he said and he opened up the first box and there inside was a bone.

'Alas!' said Ragnar Forkbeard, 'what use is a bone to us today?' But even as he spoke they heard barking and they looked over to the land, and there were a dozen dogs pulling a sledge and all staring hungrily at the bone.

And Erik said, 'This certainly was the gift we needed for today!' Then he took the second box and said, 'What can be the old Enchanter's gift for tomorrow?'

Then he opened it, and he and Ragnar Forkbeard looked inside. But all they saw was one grain of corn.

'Alas!' said Ragnar Forkbeard. 'What use will one grain of corn be to us tomorrow?' And he took the grain of corn and put it in the palm of his hand. But even as he did so a shadow fell across them, and a great white bird swooped down out of the sky and pecked up the grain of corn in its beak. Then it circled once around Golden Dragon, then twice, then a third time it circled round and then finally landed beside them on the deck. Then it turned over on its back and they saw to their amazement that the bird was roasted and ready to eat! And Erik took a knife and cut the bird in two and out fell all manner of fruit.

'This certainly is a gift for tomorrow,' said Erik, and they packed all the food up to take with them on their journey.

Then Erik helped Ragnar Forkbeard to the sledge and wrapped him in the cloak that the Enchanter's daughter had given him.

'There … now no matter what the snow and wind may do, you will be warm,' said Erik, and he put the marvellous bone on the end of a long pole and hung it in front of the dogs. Then he himself jumped onto the back of the sledge, and off they sped as fast as the wind that flew across those icy waters.

The dogs barked and ran faster and faster, chasing that marvellous bone, and the sledge whipped over the snow and Ragnar Forkbeard called out to Erik, 'I am warm and fine in this magic cloak. Are you not frozen to the marrow?'

And Erik replied, 'One hair on my head is cold, but that is all.'

And on they flew, over the ice sheet and into the frozen lands, and the sun stood a handsbreadth above the horizon.

Then Ragnar Forkbeard called out to Erik, 'I am warm and fine in this magic cloak, but the wind is icy chill and the sun will soon begin to set. Are you not frozen to the marrow?'

And Erik replied, 'One hair in my nostril is cold, but that is all,' and on they flew, over the ice-covered mountains, across crevasses and snow-filled ravines. And the wind blew chill and the sun slipped beneath the horizon.

Then Ragnar Forkbeard called out to Erik, 'I am warm in this magic cloak, but the wind cuts like a knife and the sun has gone. Are you not frozen to the marrow?'

And Erik replied, 'One hair on my leg is cold, but that is all,' and on they sped through the ice-filled night. And little by little Ragnar Forkbeard fell asleep, wrapped safely in the magic cloak.

When he awoke, the sun had climbed into the sky again, and the sledge still sped through the white winter world, and Ragnar Forkbeard called out, 'I have slept snug and fine in this magic cloak, but the night has been bitter and deathly cold. Are you not frozen to the marrow?'

And Erik replied not one word. Ragnar turned and saw Erik still standing on the sledge behind him but as stiff as rock. When he reached out his hand to touch him, he found his companion was frozen hard as ice.

Ragnar Forkbeard stopped the sledge, took his comrade in his arms, looked up at the wintry northern sun and cursed the day, and the sun hid behind a cloud.

'What shall I do?' he cried. 'Can Erik be dead?' And the tears from his eyes froze before ever they reached the ground, and lay there in the snow like pearls. 'Would that the sun had never risen today!' he cried, 'for yesterday Erik was alive and well and today he is cold as ice. And there is no man can bring back the day that is gone!'

With a heavy heart, he lay Erik down and wrapped him in the magic cloak, saying, 'At least the snow and the wind shall not touch you now.' And he took the food that they had brought and put it before him saying, 'How can I eat, when my comrade and leader is cold as death?'

But even as he spoke these words his eye fell upon something that lay in the sledge. Can you guess what it was? It was a small silver box. 'The third of the old Enchanter's gifts,' said Ragnar Forkbeard to himself. 'The gift that is for yesterday. Now, if at anytime, I truly have need of that!' And he took it, and lifted up the lid, and looked in. To his dismay the box was empty.

'Alas!' cried Ragnar Forkbeard. 'The old Enchanter's third gift, the gift that was for yesterday has been lost, and all my hopes too are fled.'

'But perhaps it is a small gift,' he said. 'A very small gift … Perhaps it is no bigger than a speck of dust …' and he put his eye right up to the box to look. As he did so, he noticed that in the lid of the box there was a mirror, and in the mirror in the lid of the box he saw his own reflection and he realised that it was talking to him. 'Ragnar Forkbeard,' it said, 'listen to me!'

'Who are you?' cried Ragnar Forkbeard.

'I am you,' said his reflection, 'but I am the you that lived yesterday, for this mirror is made of yesterday glass. Now speak to me no more, but show the mirror to Erik.'

So Ragnar Forkbeard held the mirror up to the face of his lifeless companion, and when he looked in the mirror he caught his breath, for there, in the reflection, Erik was as alive as he had been the day before.

'Hold me closer,' said Erik's reflection, and Ragnar Forkbeard held it closer to Erik's face. Then the reflection leaned forwards so that it came right out of the mirror, and put its face up against Erik's, and breathed on him. And as Ragnar Forkbeard watched, the colour began to return to Erik's cheek, then his eyelids began to tremble, and the breath returned to his body. At last his eyes opened and he smiled.

'I am back from a dream that had no beginning and no ending,' said Erik.

'You are as you were yesterday,' said his reflection. Then it withdrew, back into the mirror, and picked up a rock reflected there, and threw it straight at the mirror, and the mirror smashed to fragments, and the reflection was gone.

After that Erik and Ragnar Forkbeard loaded up the sledge once more and both wrapped themselves as best they could in the magic cloak. Then they set off upon their icy way once more.

Cold was the way and weary and many were the frozen nights they spent together, and many were the adventures that happened to them. But finally they saw, over a white hill, a puff of smoke and, when they got to the top of the hill, there below them was the camp. And there were all their comrades: Sven the Strong and Thorkhild and all the rest of them.

How Erik's men yelled and shouted for joy to see Erik and Ragnar Forkbeard alive, when they had thought them long-since dead, and to hear that Golden Dragon was safe at anchor, when they had thought her broken-up at the bottom of the sea. And how they marvelled at the tales that Erik and Ragnar Forkbeard had to tell – and especially the story of how Erik returned from the dead and of the use they had made of the old Enchanter's three wonderful gifts.

WOLF MOUNTAIN

AS LONG AS THE SNOWS covered the land, Erik and his men stayed in the camp which they had built out of logs. By day they fished and hunted. At night they would lie awake listening to the howling of the wolves outside.

'They are starving,' Erik would say to his men. 'We are lucky to be safe in our camp. A man would be torn to pieces by such a pack.'

One day Erik and Sven the Strong chased a wild boar across the frozen hills, but it escaped into a black forest.

'We dare not follow it into that place,' said Erik, 'for the sun will soon be setting and for sure that is where the wolves have their lair.'

But even as the two companions turned to head back for the camp, the sun hid behind a cloud, and they heard – in the far distance, deep in the black forest – a wolf howl. Erik shuddered, and even Sven the Strong quickened his pace as they walked away from the dark trees.

'Let us make haste,' whispered Erik.

But the snow was deep, and many was the time they sank up to their waists, and it was slow going. And behind them, in the far distance, deep in the forest, another wolf howled.

Erik turned to Sven the Strong and said, 'Let us bind these branches onto our feet so that we do not sink into the snow.' This they did, but still the way was steep and the snow too soft, and many was the time they sank up to their chests, and it was slow going.

And behind them, in the far distance, deep in the forest, another wolf howled.

Then Erik turned to Sven the Strong and said, 'Let us cut across the mountainside. It may be harder, but it will be shorter.' So they turned towards the dark mountain, and struggled on through the snow.

As the way got steeper, the snow turned to ice, and many was the time they slipped and fell, but the fearful thought of those starving wolves spurred them on.

All at once a mist descended on the mountainside, and they could not see which way they were going and behind them, nearer now, they could hear one, two … three hungry wolves howling.

'I fear they have picked up our scent,' said Erik. 'We are lost in this mist and for certain we shall never reach camp, nor see our comrades again.'

But even as he spoke, a dark shape rose up in front of them out of the mist. It was a great grey wolf – as tall as a man.

Sven the Strong raised his bow, but before he could let his arrow fly, Erik put out his hand and spoke, 'Who are you, wolf?'

But the great grey wolf did not reply. Its eyes gleamed, and it bared its great yellow teeth and snarled.

'Who are you, wolf? And what is your business with us?' said Erik.

Then the wolf snarled again and finally it said, 'Who am I? … Who are you? Do you not know that this is Wolf Mountain, and here you must obey the Law of the Wolves?'

At these words Sven the Strong raised his bow again, saying, 'That I will never do! For the Law of the Wolves is to tear each other to pieces!'

The great grey wolf lifted up its grizzled head and howled, and all around they heard the answering howls of other wolves. Then the wolf looked at Erik and Sven and said, 'That is not the Law of the Wolves. And on Wolf Mountain, if you do not know the Law of the Wolves, you will be torn to pieces.'

'But what is the Law of the Wolves?' cried Erik.

'If you do not obey it, you will die,' said the great grey wolf, and just then the mist seemed to grow thicker, until Erik and Sven could scarcely see it, and then, suddenly, the mist cleared and the old wolf was gone.

Erik and Sven looked at each other, and then they looked behind them, and far away below them they saw dark shapes slipping out from the black forest.

'The wolves are coming to Wolf Mountain,' said Erik. 'We must be quick.'

So on they climbed, and the way got harder and steeper, and soon they were climbing with hand and foot. Then Sven the Strong took a rope and handed one end to Erik.

'Here,' said Sven, 'Tie that round your waist.' Then Sven tied the other end round his own waist, and so they continued, and when the way got even steeper, Sven was able to pull Erik up with the rope.

Not long after this they came upon a mountain goat hiding in a cleft in the rock.

'Mountain goat,' said Erik, 'you live on Wolf Mountain. Tell us what is the Law of the Wolves?'

But the mountain goat shook its head, 'I do not live on Wolf Mountain. I lost my way in the mist. But I can tell you the Law of the Wolves: it is to tear everything to pieces, to strip the land bare, and to show no mercy to any living creature. That is the Law of the Wolves.'

'Then we are dead for certain,' said Erik, 'for I cannot obey such a law.'

'No more can I,' said Sven the Strong, and the two men went on their way.

On they climbed, up and up, until all at once they came upon a black bear, crouching under a rock.

'Black bear,' said Erik, 'since you live on Wolf Mountain, tell us: what is the Law of the Wolves?'

The black bear replied, 'The Law of the Wolves is to be always hungry, and never to allow your appetite to be satisfied. I do not live here, but that is the Law of the Wolves.'

'If that is the Law of the Wolves,' said Erik, 'it is not a law for men. We shall surely die here on Wolf Mountain.' Sven the Strong nodded, and they went on their way.

On they climbed, until they came to a sheer rock face. 'Now indeed we are lost,' said Erik, 'for we cannot climb that sheer rock face. There is neither foothold nor handhold.'

'I will try,' said Sven the Strong, 'and if I succeed, I will pull you up after me.'

So Sven set off to climb the sheer rock face. Straight up he went, clutching with his fingers, and straining with all his strength to stay on the wall of rock. Higher and higher he got, as Erik watched, and below them they heard the howling of the wolves getting closer all the time. And as he heard the wolves, Sven looked down for a moment, and he saw how high he was, and how little he had to hold on to, and his foot slipped, and he clutched with his hand, but the rock face seemed to crumble at his touch, and suddenly he was plunging down towards Erik in a shower of rock and ice.

As his friend fell, Erik thought to himself, 'Is this how we shall die on Wolf Mountain?' But as it happened, instead of landing on the solid ice and rock where Erik stood, Sven the Strong landed in a drift of new-fallen snow that lay close by, and Erik ran to him, and found that his leg was broken.

Then they heard a terrible sound. The howls of the wolves were close below them and, as they listened, the howls changed from howls to frenzied barks, and they heard the bleating of the mountain goat as the starving wolves set upon the poor creature. Then Erik and Sven the Strong knew that the mountain goat had not known the Law of the Wolves.

Erik lifted Sven the Strong out of the snow, and pulled him back towards the rock face. And as he did so, they heard the wolves draw closer and closer, and they heard the black bear roaring and the wolf pack barking and snarling, and they heard the sounds of a hideous fight. Then all went still, and Erik and Sven waited and listened … until one by one, the wolves began to howl again – closer than ever.

'The black bear did not know the Law of the Wolves either,' said Erik, 'and no more do we. There is only one chance for us.'

And with these words, Erik himself began to climb the impossible sheer rock face. Straight up he went, using every niche and every notch, and he never once glanced behind him. So it was that he did not see the first dark shapes appear on the ice-sheet below them, as the wolves slunk closer and closer …

'Hurry, Erik!' called Sven the Strong, 'for I see the wolves approaching!'

But Erik neither looked down, nor looked up. He just kept climbing niche by niche and notch by notch, and the wolves began to gather in their pack on the ice sheet below.

'Hurry!' called out Sven the Strong. And Erik climbed, and the wolves drew closer. Once his foot slipped, and once his hand slipped, but up he went … up and up, and then the wolves suddenly saw Sven the Strong as he lay there on the ice with his leg broken. The wolves stopped and glared and some of them snarled, and some of them licked their lips and showed their great teeth. Sven the Strong tried to stand, but he could not, for his broken leg was limp and useless.

Then the leader of the wolf pack lifted up his head and bayed, and the others started barking and snapping, and Erik heard them as he climbed higher and higher. But still he did not look down. Then suddenly the wolves were charging across the ice towards Sven the Strong. And Sven could see their hot breath bursting in the air as they raced towards him. He could see their eyes white with madness, and as they leapt at him he could see the blood of the mountain goat and the blood of the black bear red on their fangs and smeared on their sides.

But before their claws could tear his flesh, Sven the Strong suddenly found himself hoisted up into the air, and saw the wolf pack dancing on the ground below him – leaping up – trying to reach him. He looked up, and there was Erik, pulling on the rope that joined them, with all his might and with all his main. And below, the wolves snapped and snarled their disappointment, as Sven was hauled higher and higher to where Erik stood on the top of the rock face.

When Sven reached the top, Erik pulled him to safety, and then lay exhausted.

'We are safe for the moment,' said Sven the Strong, 'but sooner or later those wolves will find another way up. You must go on without me, for I cannot move with this broken leg,' and he started to untie the rope that joined them. But Erik stopped him.

'I shall never leave you to die alone,' he said.

'Better that one of us should die than both of us,' Sven replied, and once again he started to undo the rope that joined them. But once again Erik stopped him. 'We are comrades,' he said. 'Just as this rope around our waists binds us together, so our friendship binds us one to the other with an invisible bond that cannot be broken …'

But even as he spoke, they heard a snarl and looked up, and there was the great grey wolf, tall as a man, sitting on a rock, glaring at them. And as they stared at the fearful creature, dark shapes began to rise up out of the very rock, and soon there were all the wolves that

had been on the ice-sheet below, gathered round the two men in a circle, their tongues hanging out, and their eyes watching.

'Perhaps this is all a dream from which we shall awake,' said Sven the Strong. But Erik shook his head.

'Not unless life itself is a dream,' he said. And the two friends embraced, and in their minds they took farewell of each other and of life, and waited for the wolves to tear them to pieces, limb from limb.

But they stood like that for some while. Then first Erik opened his eyes and then Sven the Strong turned to look … The wolves were all around them just as before, and the great grey wolf was sitting on the rock …

'Come on!' cried Erik, 'We are not afraid to die! For we are companions in life or death.'

And the Great Grey Wolf lifted up its head and gave a howl.

'That is how we live and hunt here on Wolf Mountain – each wolf bound to the other by invisible bonds so strong that nothing can separate us. Each of us lives and dies for his comrades. That is the Law of the Wolves.'

With these words, the wolves turned and slunk off into the gathering dusk. Erik lifted Sven the Strong up, and together they limped all the rest of the way back to camp, under the full moon and down the other side of Wolf Mountain.

A HARD QUESTION

WHEN ERIK AND SVEN the Strong returned from Wolf Mountain, they roasted a wild boar that their comrades had caught. During the feast a most curious thing happened.

The wind was howling outside and Ragnar Forkbeard was telling a story, when suddenly there came a loud knocking on the door. Erik and his men looked at one another.

'Who can that be in this deserted land?' they asked.

But the knocking came again, only this time even louder.

'Open the door,' said Erik, and one of his men, whose name was Gunnar Longshanks, stood up to do so. But Thorkhild stopped him.

'Wait!' said Thorkhild, 'for I do not believe there can be anybody knocking on the door of our cabin in this forsaken land … the snow is deep on the ground and it is pitch black night outside.'

Then the knocking came again, only this time it was so loud that all the tables shook, and the swords that hung from the walls rattled.

'I fear it is some evil spirit,' said Thorkhild, 'that wants us to let it in so that it may do some mischief.'

But Erik said, 'Thorkhild! I know you understand such things better than most, and yet this may be a visitor who needs our help. We must open the door to see.'

And just then the knocking came again, only this time so loud that the whole hut shook, and the swords that hung on the walls crashed to the floor.

Then Thorkhild shook his head, and Gunnar Longshanks opened up the door. The night was black, and the bitter wind blasted into the hall, and there stood a small girl dressed in rags.

'Bring her in!' cried Erik, 'before she dies of cold in the bitter night.'

So they brought the girl into the warm hall and closed the door against the bitter wind. And they gave her a cup of warm milk and a plateful of food and sat her before the fire to

warm herself. But the girl did not eat, and she did not drink, and when she felt the warmth of the fire she began to cry.

'Why do you not eat?' asked Erik. 'And why do you not drink? And why do you sit and weep before the warm fire?'

The ragged girl looked round at Erik and his men and then said, 'I do not eat because my father does not eat. I do not drink because my father does not drink. And I weep before the fire because – even now – my father lies out yonder in the cold snow and the bitter night.'

'Then weep no more,' said Erik, 'for we shall fetch him in.' And Ragnar Forkbeard and four others put on their cloaks.

But Thorkhild went up to Erik and said, 'Do not let them go into the darkness, for I fear if you do we may never see them again.'

Erik replied, 'This child's father lies out yonder in the snow. We must find him and bring him back.'

But Thorkhild shook his head, 'I do not know what it is I fear … but I feel something unearthly is amongst us.'

'Thorkhild,' replied Erik, 'I know that you can sense things when others cannot, and yet we must not leave this child's father to die out yonder.' And Erik turned to the ragged girl and said, 'Child, where does your father lie?'

'Out yonder,' said the girl.

'But in which direction?' asked Erik.

'Oh,' said the ragged girl, 'but a stone's throw from your door.' So Ragnar Forkbeard and the other four stepped out into the pitch black night, and the girl threw a stick onto the fire.

Some time passed, and then Sven the Strong leant upon a crutch – his broken leg bound tight in a splint – and said, 'Ragnar Forkbeard and the others have been gone too long. Perhaps they have lost their way. I shall go and search for them.' And he lit a torch and put on his cloak and so did four others.

But Thorkhild went up to him and said, 'Do not go. For I do not know what it is, but I feel something unearthly amongst us, and it is growing stronger.'

Sven the Strong clasped Thorkhild by the shoulders and said, 'Thorkhild! I know you can see things when others cannot, but we must find our comrades.' So Sven the Strong hobbled out into the pitch-black night – and the four others with him – and the ragged girl threw another stick onto the fire.

A long time passed, and still neither Ragnar Forkbeard and his companions, nor Sven the Strong and his men returned. So Erik stood up and said, 'Something is wrong. I myself will go and see what has happened to our comrades.'

But Thorkhild jumped to his feet and ran to Erik and put his arms round him and said, 'Erik, for the love that you bear me, do not go into that darkness. For there is something unearthly amongst us and it has grown fearful strong!'

'I cannot leave my comrades to die in the bitter night,' said Erik, 'I must go.'

'No!' cried Thorkhild, 'I will go!'

And before Erik could stop him he had disappeared into the pitch black night, and the rest of Erik's men followed after him.

Then Erik heard a laugh and he looked round to see the ragged girl throwing a log onto the fire.

'Why do you laugh?' asked Erik, but the girl did not reply. 'Who are you?' asked Erik, and he looked into the girl's eyes and he could see his own reflection in them, by the light of the fire, and his reflection was a skeleton. Then Erik began to believe in his mind what Thorkhild had said … that there was something unearthly amongst them.

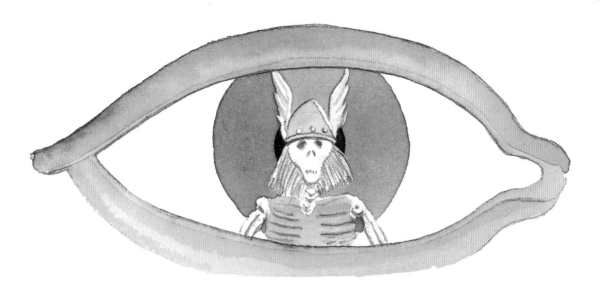

For a moment Erik hesitated, then suddenly he drew his knife and pressed it on the throat of the ragged girl, and said, 'What sort of a creature are you?'

And the girl replied, 'Would you kill a child?'

And Erik hesitated again for he did not have it in his heart to do so terrible a deed.

'But where are my men?' he asked.

'They are looking for my poor father,' said the girl. 'They will return with him at any moment.' But as she spoke, Erik could feel magic humming in the air. So he pressed his knife harder to the child's throat and said, 'Where do you come from?'

Then tears welled up in the little girl's eyes and she started to cry, and Erik put down his knife, saying to himself, 'If she were a creature of evil, surely, she could not cry like this,' and he put his arm around the girl and felt ashamed that he had threatened her. But even as he did he could feel the magic humming louder than ever in his ears.

The little girl cried and cried and Erik tried to comfort her. Finally she ceased sobbing and said, 'Fetch me some water,' and Erik ran to fetch her some water. She took the cup of water, but she did not drink it. Instead she poured it all onto the floor. And Erik watched her and wondered.

'Put more sticks on the fire,' said the girl. And Erik wondered to himself that she should order him about, and yet he said to himself, 'The poor girl must be cold,' and he put more sticks on the fire, and the magic hummed louder than ever in his ears.

'What is your name?' asked the girl.

'I cannot remember,' said Erik.

'Good,' said the girl, 'then you are entirely in my power at last!'

And Erik looked at her pale white face and he knew that he had lost his own will.

'Now take up your knife again,' said the ragged girl.

And Erik thought to himself, 'Would that I had listened to Thorkhild.' But he took up his knife.

'Now,' said the ragged girl, 'put it to your chest,' and Erik found himself obeying.

'Would that I had not sent my men away,' he thought, 'for this child has some unearthly power and I must do whatever she tells me,' and he placed his own knife on his own chest.

'Now,' said the ragged girl, 'cut out your heart and give it to me.'

'I must obey her,' said Erik to himself and he started to plunge the knife into his chest, but, before the blade had so much as pricked his skin, the ragged girl gave a cry, and Erik turned to see the smoke from the fire enveloping her.

At that moment the door burst open, and Thorkhild plunged into the smoke, and there was a scream, and then he reappeared, dragging the body not of the little ragged girl but of a troll … a wizened creature with starting eyes and its tongue hanging out. And at that moment Erik dropped his knife and now the magic had vanished.

'As soon as I saw her throwing sticks on the fire,' said Thorkhild, 'I knew there was something magic in that smoke – so when I went out I climbed on the roof of our hut and threw my cloak over the smoke hole so that the smoke would not blind me.'

Then they threw the troll's body into the snow and found Ragnar Forkbeard and his men and Sven the Strong and his men stumbling in the dark, but the smoke that had blinded them was gone too, and when they saw their comrades they embraced, and returned to the feast and vowed they would not let themselves be blinded so easily again.

'And yet,' said Erik, 'what we did was right and just. For what if the troll had been a poor ragged child – and what if she had had a father dying in the snow?'

And everyone shook their heads and agreed they did not know the answer, nor see how they should have acted otherwise. And I wonder too – what do you think?

HOW ERIK AND THANGBRAND WERE TESTED

THE WINTER WAS LONG and hard. And while the snows lay up against the walls of their hut, Erik and his men had little enough to eat, and they grew thin and sour.

'When shall we ever eat again?' they began to ask each other. 'And what of our ship, Golden Dragon? Can she still be safe, left unattended all this long time?'

Erik heard his men grumbling, one to another, but he said nothing.

Then up stood one of his men who was thinner and sourer than any of the others. His name was Thangbrand. 'Why should we put up with this any longer?' he said. 'Let us leave this place. Let us find Golden Dragon and set sail at once.' And Erik's men looked from one to the other, and then they looked at Erik. But Erik said nothing.

'Come!' said Thangbrand. 'Let us waste no more time, for if we wait any longer we shall be dead from hunger.'

'Thangbrand is right,' said Ulf Sigfusson, and he got up and stood next to Thangbrand. Then up too got Olaf Hamundson and Gunnar Longshanks and they too stood next to Thangbrand and Ulf Sigfusson. And then another got up and joined them, and another and another, until half of Erik's men were standing beside Thangbrand. Then they all looked at Erik and at last Erik spoke.

'You know my mind already. We should stay here until the snows have gone. However, if any of you wish to follow Thangbrand, I shall not stop you.'

Then some of Erik's men murmured amongst themselves, and some were astonished by Erik's words. And Thangbrand became filled with pride to think that half of Erik's men would follow him.

'But listen,' said Erik. 'We are small enough in numbers as it is. It would be certain death for only half of you to go. Either all of you must follow Thangbrand or none of you.'

Then Erik's men were even more amazed, and Thangbrand swelled even more with pride to think that all of Erik's men might follow him.

'And listen!' said Erik. 'You know that I and Ragnar Forkbeard alone have already made the journey between Golden Dragon and here, and we alone know the way and how fraught with danger it is. It would be certain death for you to go without us as well.'

Then great was the amazement amongst Erik's men, and Thangbrand puffed himself up to think that even Erik himself might follow him, and a mighty argument broke out.

At length Erik held up his hand and said, 'Since you must decide between Thangbrand and myself, let us prove which of us is the most worthy to be your leader.'

Everyone agreed to this, so Erik said, 'First let us see which of us has the strongest arm for the bow.' So Thangbrand put an arrow into his bow, and pulled back the string till it was behind his ear. Then he let his arrow fly so fast and hard that it buried itself in the trunk of an oak tree right up to its feathers.

But Erik said, 'My arrow will go straight through that oak tree and come out the other side.'

'That's impossible!' said Thangbrand.

'Not at all,' said Erik, and he pulled back his bowstring no further than his elbow and let his arrow fly straight and true.

But he did not aim at the trunk of the tree, instead he aimed at an oak apple, hanging from a branch, and the arrow split the oak apple in two and came out the other side, and embedded itself in the oak tree behind.

'Thangbrand has the stronger arm for the bow,' said Erik's men, shaking their heads, 'but Erik is the more cunning.'

Then Erik said, 'Let us see which of us is the mightier swordsman.' And he went to a tree stump and lifted his sword Blueblade high above his head, and smote the tree stump such a mighty blow that it was cleft in two right down to its roots.

Then Thangbrand went to a boulder; and swung his sword high and wild above his head, and brought it down with a crashing blow that sent sparks and flashes of iron from his sword flying in all directions. The boulder quivered, and then split in two, and Thangbrand held his battered sword up aloft in triumph. Everyone shook their heads and agreed that Thangbrand was the mightier swordsman.

'Finally,' said Erik, 'let us see which of us is the braver.' And without more words he took his bare hand and held it in the flame from the fire until the hairs on his arm began to singe and curl, and then he took it out again. Then Thangbrand smiled a broad smile, and bared his arm and plunged it into the fire right up to the shoulder. And he kept it there while the hairs on his arm began to curl and singe, and then his nails began to go black, and still he kept it there, and then his skin began to burn and at last he could bear it no longer, and with a mighty cry he pulled his arm from the flames, but already the fire had done its work and his arm hung limp and useless by his side, and he fell down fainting from the pain.

Everybody shook their heads and agreed that Thangbrand was indeed a brave man. But Erik turned to them and said, 'Yet is it possible that any of you were prepared to follow this man? He has certainly a strong arm for the bow, but he has no cunning. He may be a mighty swordsman, but now he has no sword. And what is worst of all, his foolish pride has cost him his good fighting arm. How far would you have got following such a man on such a journey none of you knew whither?

'I am not your leader because I have the strongest arm for the bow, or the mightiest sword, or even the bravest heart, but because you have learned to trust my judgement, and know that even when I am wrong I speak for the good of us all and not for pride.'

After that, all the men returned to their places. Thangbrand lay sick on his bed for many days and never fully recovered the use of his right arm and was ever after called Thangbrand One-Hand. And Erik and his men stayed safe in their camp until the snow and the winter were past.

ERiK AND THE GREAT BiRD

WHEN THE WINTER WAS OVER, Erik and his men set off on the long journey to find their ship, Golden Dragon. As they journeyed, Ragnar Forkbeard looked around him, 'This is a fine country,' he said. 'A man could lead a good life here if he chose.'

No sooner were the words out of his lips than a cloud came across the sun. And Erik and his men looked up to see – flying slowly through the air – the most monstrous bird that any of them had ever seen. It was black, and it was as big as six ships in full sail.

'Quick!' said Erik, and they dived behind a rock as the vast creature swooped down over them. And the tips of its wings seemed to brush the ground on either side of them, and a cloud of dust flew up and the draught of air from its wings was like a gale that threw them on their faces and left them gasping for breath.

As it passed over them they could see it had a huge razor-sharp beak and its claws were like iron hooks, and there was not one of Erik's band who was not filled with an unutterable fear.

When it had gone, Erik stepped out from the rock and said, 'Let us make haste.'

But some of his men said, 'No, we dare not go another inch!'

'Are you mad?' replied Erik. 'Do you think you can spend the rest of your lives behind that rock?' So one by one they came out, gazing fearfully up at the sky. 'Now,' said Erik, 'we must keep our eyes open for that monster, and stay near cover as we travel.'

And on they went, many of them still trembling with fear.

At last they came to an open plain. 'What shall we do now?' they asked each other. 'We must cross this plain where there is neither rock nor tree to give us shelter nor any hole to hide in. If the great bird returns while we are crossing such a place, it will snap us up as easily as worms off a plate!'

Erik stared across the plain, and he knew that they were right. Nevertheless, he shrugged his shoulders and said, 'We have no choice.'

'Let us return to our camp,' said some of his men. 'At least we can be safe there.'

'And live the rest of our lives in terror and hiding?' asked Erik.

'At least that is better than being eaten alive by that monster,' they replied.

But even as they spoke they heard a terrible noise, and on the far horizon they saw a black shape rising into the sky. Quaking with fear, Erik and his men hid once more. And if the bird had seemed gigantic before, it now seemed like a great thundercloud blotting out half the sky. And it wheeled overhead and swooped down over their hiding-place as if it knew they were there. And as it came low they could smell the strong bird-smell that clung to its talons.

'If we'd been out on that plain now,' muttered Sven the Strong, 'we would certainly have been snapped up as easily as worms off a plate … each and every one of us!'

'Caw – Caw' screeched the bird, and its voice was like a thunderclap that made the rocks shake and the earth tremble.

'I can't hide away like a rabbit!' cried Ragnar Forkbeard. 'I will slay this crow!' and before anyone could stop him, he'd leapt out of the cleft of rock in which they were hiding and aimed his bow, strong and true, and let fly an arrow that struck the creature in its claw.

'CAW – CAW!' screeched the bird, and wheeled round in the sky and swooped low over where Ragnar Forkbeard was standing, and snatched him up in its monstrous claw, and then flew off over the great plain and beyond the furthest region.

The men were silent for some moments after this. Then Erik spoke: 'Now we cannot go back. We must find our comrade!'

'But what can we do?' moaned some of his men.

'I do not know,' said Erik.

'How can we hide from that monster, if we cross that open plain?' they cried.

'I do not know,' said Erik, and put his head in his hands. Then Thorkhild whispered to Erik, 'We must go!' and together they set off across that wide open plain in the direction the great bird had taken.

'It may be useless,' said Sven the Strong, 'but I cannot see them go alone,' and he followed after them. One or two followed him and then more and then no one was left behind. In this manner they walked for a mile across the open plain, expecting at any moment the great monster to darken the sky once more.

But they walked another mile and still there was no sign of the great bird. And after another mile, Thorkhild said, 'Who knows? Perhaps we shall make it safely across the plain after all.'

'Ssh!' said Erik. 'Look!' He pointed, and in the distance they could just see some mountains rising out of the ground. 'If we can make it to those mountains, we shall be safe.' So, keeping their eyes on the sky, they quickened their pace.

But they hadn't gone more than a few yards before one of Erik's men yelled out, 'There it is again!' And they all threw themselves to the ground but, when they looked up, they saw it was not the great bird at all – just a black cloud scudding across the sun.

On they went once more, and eventually they reached the mountains, and found themselves beside a rocky stream. 'We shall be safe now,' said Erik. 'Let us follow this stream, and perhaps it will take us to where the great bird lives, and there, perhaps, we will be able to kill it when it is asleep.'

Without more ado, Erik put his foot in the water, but the moment he did so there was a cackle of laughter, and he looked up and saw a curious creature sitting in a tree.

'Who are you?' asked Erik. 'And what are you laughing at?'

'I am the spirit of that stream you're standing in,' said the creature, 'and I always laugh,' and it opened its wide mouth and it laughed a laugh like the tinkling of water in a brook.

Erik looked at his men, but they were talking earnestly amongst themselves.

'You're the only one that can see me!' laughed the spirit of the stream. 'And then, only while you're standing in the water. What do you want with me?'

'I want you to take me to where the great bird lives,' replied Erik.

Again the spirit of the stream opened its wide mouth and laughed a laugh like the tumbling of waterfalls. 'There is no great bird,' it said.

'But we have seen it … twice!' cried Erik.

'Don't believe everything you see!' smiled the spirit of the stream.

'And we have felt the wind from its wings on our faces,' said Erik.

'Don't believe everything you feel!' laughed the spirit of the stream.

'And it has carried away our comrade, Ragnar Forkbeard!' cried Erik.

The spirit of the stream stopped laughing, and looked at Erik and said, 'There is no great bird. It is something inside you that has taken wing, and it will continue to carry off your comrades until you find out what it is.'

Then the spirit of the stream opened its mouth wider than ever and laughed a laugh like the breaking of oceans, and then climbed into its own mouth and disappeared. Erik sat down on the edge of the stream with his head in his hands. 'Now I fear we shall never see Ragnar Forkbeard again … for how can that great bird be something inside me? And even it if were – how could I even begin to find out what it was?'

Then Thorkhild knelt down beside Erik and asked, 'What have you seen that troubles you so?'

And Erik replied, 'I have seen the end of our hopes. I have seen that we shall never reach Golden Dragon nor find the land where the sun goes at night.'

'Erik,' said Thorkhild, 'you must not say such things for – even if they are true – how could we follow you, knowing you believed them?'

'Thorkhild,' replied Erik, 'you are right.' Then he turned to the others and said, 'Come! Let us find our comrade, Ragnar Forkbeard,' and they all moved on up the mountain stream.

They climbed higher and higher, and then all at once they rounded a corner and found themselves confronted by a dark forest.

'How strange,' muttered Erik, 'to find a forest so high up a mountainside.' Nevertheless, he led his men straight into the gloomy depths. They hadn't gone far, however, before they found their way blocked. In front of them the trees no longer stood upright, but lay horizontal, piled one on top of the other, up as high as the men could see.

'Who has ever seen a forest like this?' asked Sven the Strong.

'We must climb up, and see what we can see,' said Erik.

'I do not like this,' murmured more than one of Erik's men as they climbed. 'Who knows how this forest came to be like this?'

But Erik told them to be quiet, and up they climbed, until at last they reached the top. And there a most extraordinary sight met their eyes: the pile of horizontal trees stretched out in a great circle, half a mile wide, in the shape of a basin.

'Don't you see where we are!' cried Erik.

'I've never seen such a thing,' said Sven the Strong, 'and it means nothing to me.'

'We are in the nest of the great bird!' cried Erik. 'And see! Who is that small figure in the middle?'

They all looked and saw, down in the bottom of the great bird's nest, amongst the threaded trunks of trees, their comrade whom they thought was lost, Ragnar Forkbeard.

'Is he alive or dead?' they asked each other, and then they saw him scramble to his feet and wave at them.

Erik turned to Thorkhild and said, 'Now I truly believe that we shall find Golden Dragon and that we shall reach our final goal.'

Then without another thought, they all ran down into the great nest of trees, jumping from trunk to trunk, until they had reached their comrade. And there they hugged and clapped each other on the back.

'But we must make haste,' said Thorkhild. 'We are right in the middle of the great bird's nest, it might return at any moment!'

'Indeed it might!' said Ragnar Forkbeard, 'and yet the curious thing is that it did not harm me. Its talons were great and strong and yet it scarcely scratched the surface of my skin.'

'We can take our time,' said Erik, 'the bird will not return.'

'But how can you be so sure?' asked his men.

'That I may not tell you,' replied Erik, 'but, as I am your leader, you can believe what I say.'

And so they took their way out of the great bird's nest and down the mountain, and set off once more in search of Golden Dragon.

That night, as they lay down to sleep, Thorkhild took Erik on one side and said, 'Erik, what made you so certain that the great bird would not return?'

Erik swore Thorkhild to secrecy and then told him what the spirit of the stream had said. 'But it was you, Thorkhild, who made me see what it was within me. There was no great bird, as the spirit of the stream said, but it was the doubt that had grown in my mind, taking wing and casting a cloud over all of us.'

Thorkhild shook his head. 'This is a fine country,' he said, 'and a man could lead a good life here, but you cannot live for long in a land in which there is no room for doubt.'

'No,' said Erik, 'let us get away from here as soon as we are able.'

So they slept, and the next day they set off to find their ship.

THE TALKING VALLEY

ERIK AND HIS MEN travelled on until they came to a green valley full of blue flowers. Thorkhild sniffed the breeze and said, 'There is something curious about this valley.'

But they set off across it, until they came to a tree leaning over a clear pool. 'I have never seen such a tree before,' said Erik. 'Look! Its bark is lined with gold!'

'So it is!' cried his men, and they seized their knives and began to strip out the gold from the bark of the tree. But suddenly a gentle voice stopped them. 'Don't!' it said.

Erik and his men looked all around them, but they could see no one, so they shrugged and carried on. And then the gentle voice spoke again. 'Don't!' it said, 'for I will die.'

Erik and his men looked at each other. Then they looked behind the tree, and then they looked in its branches.

'I must be dreaming!' said Erik. 'But it seemed to me as if the tree spoke.'

'How can a tree speak?' cried Sven the Strong, and he took his knife again, and began to strip out more gold from the bark.

'Do not kill me,' said the gentle voice once more.

'Who are you?' cried Sven the Strong, letting go of his knife.

'I am the tree that you are wounding with your sharp blade,' replied the voice.

'What sort of country is this,' cried Erik, 'where trees can speak?'

'This is the Talking Valley,' replied the tree. 'In it you will find many wonderful things, but you can do much harm.'

'What sort of tree are you?' asked Erik.

'I am a Stone Tree,' replied the tree. 'My bark is seamed with gold, my branches are shot through with silver, and my leaves are veined with fine filigree, but all my fruits are stones, and when summer ends my back is almost broken by their weight.'

'But how is it you can speak?' asked Ragnar Forkbeard.

'I can speak no more nor less than any tree,' replied the Stone Tree. 'It is just that you can understand, for all who touch the gold from my bark can ever after understand all plants.'

'Is that true, grass?' asked Erik.

'It's true!' whispered a million tiny voices, and a million blades of grass waved together in the wind.

'But this is more wonderful than anything I have ever seen or heard before!' exclaimed Ragnar Forkbeard, and he bent down and heard a daisy singing in a high voice:

'I am bowing to the sun

And when my day is done

I shall turn away and wait

For my friend to come, to come.'

'Daisy!' whispered Ragnar Forkbeard. 'We are seeking the land where the sun goes at night. Since the sun is your friend, do you know where it is?'

And the daisy replied, 'I am only a daisy, living down here in this valley – why don't you ask the trailing vine that grows on the hill? He's sure to know.'

So Ragnar Forkbeard went to the hill and spoke to the trailing vine, which was clinging to a rock, and the vine replied, 'I grow up here and have a fine view over this valley … I see that all the flowers and all the trees are in their proper places … and that's a heavy responsibility, as you can well understand …'

'But do you know the land where the sun goes at night, vine?' asked Ragnar Forkbeard. 'Come to the point.'

'I like to go in all directions,' replied the vine, 'and take my time … but right now I'm climbing up this rock … perhaps in a year or two I'll be able to look over the top, and then I'll be able to answer your question …'

'But we know!' said some voices from higher up, and Ragnar Forkbeard looked up to see some of the blue flowers, which filled the valley, waving down to him.

'Don't believe those orchids,' said the vine, 'they're full of tricks and they don't like strangers.'

But Ragnar Forkbeard had already climbed up to the blue orchids. 'Tell me,' he said, 'what you know.'

'Take one of my petals, and eat it,' said the blue flower nearest to him. So Ragnar

Forkbeard broke off a petal, and a hush went over all the orchids. Then he ate the petal and waited. But nothing happened. 'Well?' said Ragnar Forkbeard, but the blue orchids said nothing to him. So Ragnar Forkbeard turned back to the vine and said: 'Why do the orchids say nothing?' But the vine was also silent. Then Ragnar Forkbeard suddenly knew that the magic power to hear and understand all plants had left him and that he had been tricked by the blue orchids.

Meanwhile Erik and the others were still standing round the Stone Tree. Sven the Strong broke off a branch and sure enough, just as the tree had said, it was shot through with silver.

And while Sven was holding it, he heard a shout: 'Run! Run! Run for your lives!' and he turned round and saw three hares racing across the meadow. And the biggest of the hares was calling to the others, 'Run, little brothers! Run!'

'What is it you hear, Sven?' asked Erik, and he took the silver-lined branch from Sven's hand, and then he too heard the hares calling to each other, and he heard a buzzard high up in the sky crying, 'Run, little hares! Save yourselves for me!' Then a fox appeared from the wood, and glared up at the buzzard, crying, 'They're mine buzzard! Mine!' and he raced after the hares.

And Erik's men passed the silver branch from one to another, and whoever touched it could from then on understand not only plants but the animals as well.

'Stone Tree!' said Erik, 'your bark makes us hear plants speaking, your branches make us understand the language of animals … now tell us … what do your leaves do?'

And the Stone Tree replied, 'Do not hurt me further, for everything you take from me is a little death.'

'But you'll soon grow new leaves!' cried Erik.

'Alas … no,' said the Stone Tree, 'I am not like other trees. My fruit are stones, which break my back with their weight, and I cannot grow anything else.'

But one of Erik's men had already broken off a leaf, and the Stone Tree sighed and said, 'Drop it in the pool and then taste the water.'

And when they did … can you guess what happened? They heard the pool chuckling in a deep, cool voice, 'So you're looking for the land where the sun goes at night.'

'How do you know, pool?' asked Erik.

'Because,' said the pool, 'the rocks told me.'

And Erik and his men heard the rocks say, 'We heard it from the vine.'

'Now,' said Thorkhild, 'we can understand the plants and the wild beasts and even the very earth itself!'

'And perhaps now,' said Erik, 'we shall also learn something of the land where the sun goes at night.'

But before he had finished speaking a terrific noise filled their ears.

'Ah!' said the pool, 'the trees of the forest are beginning their choir practice. They usually do about this time.' And at once all the stones started chattering away with excitement, and the grass giggled, and the birds shouted and yelled at the trees.

'This is indeed the Talking Valley!' exclaimed Erik, and for the rest of the day he and his men wandered through the valley marvelling at the thousands of voices that they heard, and listening to the birds and the insects, the fish in the stream, the reeds at the water's edge, and the water itself and even the sticks and stones that lay by the wayside.

Only Ragnar Forkbeard remained on his own. He did not tell anyone that he had lost the power to hear those wonderful things, but he set himself on guard over the baggage and equipment.

Many days passed, and Erik and his men never tired of listening to the Talking Valley. Indeed they scarcely noticed how the days were passing. But at length Erik came to Thorkhild and said, 'I am troubled.'

'Have you grown tired of the Talking Valley so soon?' asked Thorkhild.

'No,' answered Erik, 'but it troubles me that our ship, Golden Dragon, is lying unguarded in some foreign bay.'

'Listen!' said Thorkhild, 'the mountains are shouting to each other across the valley!'

'And it troubles me,' went on Erik, 'that while we stay in the Talking Valley here, we are forgetting our quest: to find the land where the sun goes at night.'

'Listen!' said Thorkhild, 'the frogs are telling each other jokes and the stream is singing a new song!'

At this Erik wandered away from Thorkhild lost in thought.

Then Erik called all his men together and said, 'We must leave this Valley of Talk and find our ship Golden Dragon.'

But the men were not listening to him. They were listening to the trees and creatures calling from the dark wood.

'We must carry on with our quest!' shouted Erik, but it was no use. The men had already wandered away, and he stood there on his own. Then it was that he came across Ragnar Forkbeard sitting on guard.

'How is it, Ragnar Forkbeard, that you alone pay no attention to all that the plants and animals and stones are saying?' asked Erik.

So Ragnar Forkbeard told Erik what he had told to no one else – how he had been tricked by the orchids, and he hung his head, expecting Erik to laugh. But Erik did not laugh.

'Perhaps you have saved us all, Ragnar Forkbeard!' he said.

'Saved us all from what?' asked Ragnar Forkbeard.

'From wasting the rest of our lives away in this Valley of Talk,' replied Erik.

And he ran to the blue orchids and tore off as many petals as he could and crushed them into the mead that they all drank that night. And the next day they woke up as men from a dream.

'Did the flowers really sing yesterday?' they asked each other. 'Is it really possible that the hills were talking to us last night?'

Then they went on their way, and Erik did not tell them what he had done, until they were many miles away from the Talking Valley. And when Erik finally told them, the men grumbled and said he had taken away from them the most wonderful gift anyone had ever possessed.

'But what good is such a gift to us?' replied Erik. 'If it stops us being ourselves, it is as useless as the fruits of the Stone Tree itself. We are men, and we must do what we set out to do.'

And so they went on their way, and came to the bay where Golden Dragon lay at anchor.

THE SPELL-HOUND

WHEN AT LAST THEY REACHED their ship, Golden Dragon, Erik and his men gave a great shout of joy. But as the echo of it died, Thorkhild said, 'Did you see that thing?'

'What thing?' asked Erik.

I thought I saw a black creature looking over the side of our ship …' said Thorkhild, but the others shook their heads.

When they reached Golden Dragon, Erik said, 'Take care, for sometimes Thorkhild sees things which we do not see.' But when they searched the boat, they found nothing, and so they set sail without more ado.

Scarcely had the ship left the bay, however, than Thorkhild gave a cry, and they all turned and saw a great black dog standing at the helm of the ship.

'Look at its eyes!' cried Thorkhild, and they all saw that in its glowing yellow eyes, it had no pupils.

'Is it blind?' asked Erik, but no one could tell, and the dog neither barked nor moved. It merely stood there at the helm, and the tiller seemed to move of its own accord.

'This is no mortal dog,' said Thorkhild, 'this is a spell-hound!' And there was not one amongst them that dared go near the helm, as long as that black dog stood there.

The wind blew and Golden Dragon sped through the seas, with the black dog at the tiller until at last Thorkhild turned to Erik and said, 'I have heard my grandfather tell of such a dog boarding ships in the far long ago. Sometimes it would steer a ship to an island, where they found unimaginable treasure. But sometimes it would steer a ship over the edge of the world.'

'How can we tell which way this spell-hound will steer us?' asked Ragnar Forkbeard.

'That I do not know,' replied Thorkhild.

Erik was silent for a while, and Golden Dragon sped on through the salt spray, while the black dog stood, unmoving, by the tiller. And Erik's men whispered one to the other, 'We are heading for the edge of the world!'

Then Erik spoke. 'We shall not be steered anywhere by such a creature!' he said.

'How do we get rid of it?'

'That also I do not know,' replied Thorkhild.

Then Erik stood up and walked across the deck and boldly began to address the spell-hound. But Thorkhild gripped Erik by the arm and said, 'Do not speak to it … for one thing I do know is that once you speak to it you will be in its power.'

But Erik said, 'Even now we are all in its power, and we don't know which way we are speeding!' And with that he turned to the dog and shouted out, 'Spell-hound! Do you hear me?'

The spell-hound replied, 'There is only one question that I may answer, and that is not it …' and it growled a deep growl, and suddenly leapt down from the helm and stood over Erik with its ugly teeth bared.

'Do not ask it any more questions,' whispered Thorkhild, 'for I fear it will pick you up and toss you into the sea like a dead rat!' But Erik could no longer hear Thorkhild, for all he could hear was the deep growl in the spell-hound's throat.

But Erik stood firm and said to the dog, 'Spell-hound! Where are you steering us?'

The black dog half-closed its blind eyes and gave an even deeper growl and replied, 'There is only one question that I may answer, and that is not it …' And it bent down and picked Erik up in its teeth just as if he had been a dead rat, as Thorkhild had said.

'Put me down!' cried Erik, and he drew his sword, Blueblade, and struck the creature on the nose, but the moment the steel touched the creature, Blueblade leapt from out of Erik's hands, and flew up to the top of the mast, where it stuck fast.

'Stop!' cried Thorkhild to Erik. 'Ask him no more!' But Erik could not hear him … all he could hear was the deep growl in the spell-hound's throat, and all he could feel was its hot breath on his skin, and all he could see was its bright sightless eyes, burning into him.

'Spell-hound!' cried Erik. 'Why are you here?'

And the spell-hound growled an even deeper growl and replied, 'There is only one question I may answer, and that's not it! And now I shall throw you so high in the air that you will never come down, neither here nor there.' And it started to twirl Erik round and round in its mouth just as if he had been a dead rat.

'Do something, Thorkhild!' cried out Ragnar Forkbeard. 'Surely there is something we can do!' And at the same time the rest of Erik's men leapt to their feet, and ran at the great dog with their swords, but just as had happened before, the moment they touched it with their blades, their swords flew out of their hands and straight up into the air, and stuck into the top of the mast. And all the while the spell-hound twirled Erik around faster and faster. And Ragnar Forkbeard cried out, 'Thorkhild, what is the question? Quick!'

And Thorkhild closed his eyes and said, 'I don't know! I don't know!'

Then suddenly Sven the Strong yelled out, 'Spell-hound!' and the dog stopped twirling Erik round, and laid its ears back like a dog who hears a command. 'Who is your master?' cried out Sven.

And the black dog dropped Erik to the deck and put its tail between its legs and said, 'There is only one question that I may answer and that is it. And it is written on the silver collar round my neck.'

So Sven the Strong leapt to its side, and grabbed it by the collar and read the name there and then called out, 'Al-Kwasarmi! O, Magician! Call your dog home!' and with that the spell-hound turned a somersault where it crouched, and then another, and soon it was spinning like a Catherine Wheel. And then it rolled along the deck and off across the waves and disappeared over the most distant horizon.

Erik picked himself up and the others crowded round him. But no sooner was he on his feet than they heard the most terrible roaring sound that any of them had ever heard and Erik turned to Sven and said, 'You have saved my life, but I fear it is too late … for by that roaring it sounds to me as if we have already reached the Edge of the World …'

AT THE EDGE OF THE WORLD

1. THE ARRIVAL

AS SOON AS ERIK had said these words, they all turned and saw a blackness in the sky, and all the time the roaring got louder and louder. And the sea started running faster and faster, until it was running like some vast river towards the edge of an unimaginable waterfall.

'To the oars!' cried Erik, and his men seized their oars and rowed with all their might, but it made not a scrap of difference.

'We shall be swept over the edge without any doubt!' thought each man to himself.

Then Ragnar Forkbeard shouted out to Thorkhild, 'Thorkhild! What lies beyond the Edge of the World?' But Thorkhild just bent his head to his oar and shrugged. So Ragnar Forkbeard called out to Erik, 'Erik! What lies beyond the Edge of the World?' But Erik just bent his head to his oar and shrugged. Then Ragnar Forkbeard turned to the rest and yelled above the roaring of the waters, 'Does anyone know what lies beyond the Edge of the World?' But they all just bent their heads to their oars and shrugged. Then Ragnar Forkbeard yelled out with all his strength, for the roaring of the waters was growing louder every second, 'Then why are we so afraid? Since we don't know what there is to be afraid of!'

At this Thorkhild turned to Ragnar Forkbeard and said, 'That is often the very thing that people are most afraid of, Ragnar Forkbeard.' And he too put his head down and rowed. But Ragnar Forkbeard cried out, 'Throw me that rope!'

'What use will that be?' said Sven the Strong, and would not move from his oar.

So Ragnar Forkbeard leapt across the ship and seized the rope himself.

'What are you doing, Ragnar Forkbeard' cried Erik. 'We need everyone to bend his back to his oar!' But Ragnar Forkbeard did not reply … he tied a loop in the rope, and threw it

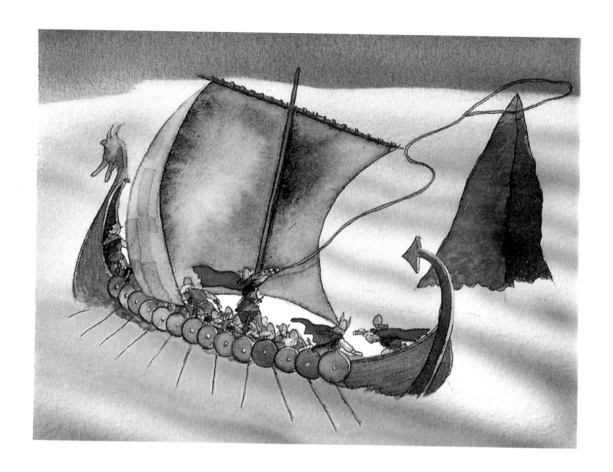

strong and true so that it landed round a rock that was sticking up in the sea like a dragon's tooth. And immediately the rope went taut and the ship stopped, while the waters swirled past towards the Edge of the World.

When everyone realised what had happened, they put up their oars and hung their heads, and Erik said, 'Look at us! We were all so filled with the fear of the unknown that we did not look for ourselves, and we did not see that rock that sticks up out of the sea like a dragon's tooth. Ragnar Forkbeard alone kept his head!'

'But we are not saved yet!' replied Ragnar Forkbeard. 'We cannot stay here tied to this rock for the rest of our lives!'

'What shall we do?' cried the rest of Erik's men, while the sea hurtled past the boat, tearing and buffeting the wooden vessel.

'We will do the only thing we can,' replied Erik. 'We shall pay a visit to the Edge of the World!'

2. THE WATERFALL OF SEAS

WHEN ERIK SAID THIS, his men looked at each other in disbelief. 'Has our leader gone mad?' they asked. But Erik spoke again, 'Since we cannot row against the sea, let us go wherever it takes us.' But some of his men fell on their knees and begged him to let them stay where they were. 'Who knows?' they said, 'somebody may rescue us before we die …'

'No,' said Erik, 'I will not stay here, tied to this rock that sticks up out of the sea like a dragon's tooth, a moment longer! Besides, I'd like to see the Edge of the World so I can tell my wife about it when I get home.' And some of his men fell on their faces, they were so terrified. 'Put us out on the rock that sticks out of the sea like a dragon's tooth,' they cried. 'We would rather take our chance there – such as it is – than go to the Edge of the World!'

But Erik only laughed out loud. 'Don't worry!' he said, 'You can shiver where you are on your own benches, for I plan to take a look at the Edge of the World alone and then return to tell you all about it.'

So saying he launched the small rowing boat, fastening its stern to the prow of Golden Dragon by a long, long rope. Then he jumped in and turned to wave goodbye, but as he did so, Sven the Strong jumped down beside him.

'I cannot let you go all alone to see such a wonderful sight as the Edge of the World! I'll come with you and be your witness!' said Sven the Strong. And so the sea carried the little boat with Erik and Sven the Strong towards the Edge of the World.

'Take care the rope doesn't break!' shouted Thorkhild. But they could not hear a word, for the roaring of the water and the rushing of the sea was so loud in their ears.

The ocean current pulled the boat this way and that way, and Sven sat in front, peering through the spray, while Erik slowly paid out the rope that held them back.

'The spray and the mist are so thick,' called out Sven the Strong, 'that I shall not be able to tell when we reach the Edge of the World!' But Erik kept on paying out the line, and the roaring got louder and louder, and the little boat pulled at its rope harder and harder … and they knew they must be getting closer and closer to the Edge of the World.

Then suddenly they came through the spray and the mist, and the most amazing sight greeted their eyes. There was the sea stretching out on either side of them, but suddenly plunging vertically downwards, like a vast waterfall that stretched from one horizon to the other.

In front of them the sky stretched on down and down below them until it merged into blackness, and there they saw stars at their feet, and below the stars nothing but a blackness that never ended. Erik payed out a little more rope and the little boat strained against the headlong waters, and inched its nose over the edge. Sven the Strong leaned over the prow and peered down.

'What do you see?' cried Erik. But Sven the Strong did not reply. He pulled himself back into the boat and turned to Erik and he was as white as a sheet.

'Hold the rope!' shouted Erik, 'I want to see for myself.' But Sven the Strong stopped him.

'Don't,' he said, 'what good can it do?'

'But I must look – now we've come so far!' shouted Erik above the thundering waters.

'When I looked over, I felt my strength draining away from me,' replied Sven the Strong. 'It was being sucked down over that fearful edge as fast as these waters plunge into the dark.'

'Take the rope!' cried Erik. 'I must look for myself.' And he thrust the rope into Sven's hands and leaned over the prow and peered down over the Edge of the World. There was the void. Nothing but blackness below them, and oceans plunging straight down into it – until they were lost to sight. And just as Sven had said, Erik too felt his strength draining away, tumbling with the pell-mell sea into the abyss. Erik's heart began to pound and his mind began to reel. 'Nothing,' he thought, 'could be so immense, so deep and so empty!'

Just then Sven the Strong gave a cry, 'My strength has gone!' he shouted, 'I cannot hold on!' And as he said the words, the rope slipped through his hands and the little rowing boat with the two men in it shot out into the black abyss, thrown by the force of the water. Erik gripped the sides with all his might, and Sven clung on for dear life, but the oars flew up and then plummeted down, down, slowly down into the blackness below and were gone forever. And Erik watched them … fascinated … as if he were more concerned for their fate than for his own.

But at that moment the boat itself began to fall, and the two men clung on desperately. Then, with a wrench, it reached the end of the rope that Erik had tied to the stern.

And his knot held and the sternpost creaked, but that too held. And the rope tore and many strands broke loose and ravelled up under the strain, but that too held and the boat fell back and dangled there over the abyss, with the wall of falling ocean crashing down upon it and the two men, scarcely able to breathe, unable to see and almost battered senseless.

Then quite suddenly all went quiet. Erik shook the water from his face, and opened his eyes. It was dark, and yet behind him the wall of water continued to fall. Then gently he nudged Sven the Strong and said, 'See what has happened to us!'

'Where are we?' cried Sven.

'Don't you see what's happened?' cried Erik. 'We've gone right through the Waterfall of Seas and have come out the other side. We are under the lip of the Edge of the World!'

By this time their eyes were becoming accustomed to the dark, and they could see that they were in a cave that ran like a tunnel in both directions as far as they could see, with the falling water making one wall.

'Look!' said Erik to Sven the Strong. 'Do you see what I see?'

And Sven the Strong looked.

'Do you see? There inside is a pool!' cried Erik. And Sven looked and looked and then he too could see that the cavern opened up behind them, and there within it was a great lake.

'Now!' said Erik, 'we have our way before us!'

'I don't understand,' replied Sven the Strong.

'I mean,' said Erik, 'that we must set Golden Dragon afloat upon that lake. For since we can go neither backwards nor forwards in the world above, we shall explore the underworld here. Who knows what we may find? Or where this water will lead us?'

Sven the Strong went silent for a moment. Then he closed his eyes and shook his head, and said, 'We can't!'

'We can't do anything else!' replied Erik.

'But how can we get back to Golden Dragon?' asked Sven the Strong.

'We must climb back up the rope over the Edge of the World,' said Erik.

3. THE DRAGON'S TOOTH

SVEN THE STRONG felt sick in the pit of his stomach, for he dreaded to look again into the black abyss that lay beyond the Edge of the World, but he said to Erik, 'Let me try first.' And without more words, he took hold of the rope that still ran from the rowing boat back up through the Waterfall of Seas to Golden Dragon. But Erik pulled him back. Then he tied another line around Sven's waist and held the other end himself.

'Good luck, Sven,' said Erik.

So Sven the Strong began to climb the ravelling rope back up over the Edge of the World.

But once he was back in the pounding waterfall, he could not see and he could not breathe, and the weight of the water falling upon him was more than any man could bear, and his hands began to slip, and his lungs filled with water so that he could not even shout as suddenly he fell back down, and Erik only just saw his body hurtle past in the deluge, and only just had time to brace himself before the rope went taut, and he too felt the force of the Waterfall of Seas dragging him down.

Erik got a foothold behind a ledge of rock and pulled and strained with all his might, until at last he pulled the limp body of Sven the Strong out of the pitching water. At first he thought his comrade was dead, but shortly Sven moaned and stirred, and opened his eyes.

'If you could not climb up through the Waterfall of Seas and back over the Edge of the World,' said Erik, 'no man could.'

'Then we shall never see our comrades nor Golden Dragon again,' said Sven, and he put his head in his hands.

But Erik said 'Ssh!' and he stood with his head on one side. 'Do you hear what I hear?'

Sven the Strong joined him and he too listened.

'What do you hear?' whispered Erik.

'Nothing,' said Sven, 'except the breaking of the waves far far away.'

'But that's it!' cried Erik. 'There are no waves down here!' And at that moment he stopped in his tracks and pointed up at the roof of the cavern. And when Sven the Strong looked he saw a narrow shaft going straight up through the solid rock and at the very top, a pin-prick of light, and down the shaft came the distant sound of waves breaking on a rock.

Then Sven the Strong lifted Erik to the cave's roof, and Erik put his back up against one side of the shaft and his feet against the other, and in this way began to climb the narrow shaft towards the pin-prick of light.

As he got higher and higher, he did not dare to look below, for the shaft went straight down, and if he slipped he would surely be dashed to pieces on the rocks below. But he kept his eyes fixed on that point of light above him, which was getting bigger all the time. The shaft was smooth and straight and had neither foothold nor handhold, and once his foot slipped, and once he thought he was too exhausted and weak to carry on, but eventually he placed his hand into the hole of light, and pulled himself out into the day.

And then he could hardly believe his eyes, for he found himself gazing out from the very pinnacle of the very rock that stuck out of the sea like a dragon's tooth, to which Ragnar Forkbeard had tied their ship. And there was Golden Dragon herself, still pulling on the rope that secured her.

'Of course!' cried Erik. 'A dragon's tooth is sharp and long but it is also always hollow! This rock is indeed a true dragon's tooth!'

Then he waved to his men and they could scarcely believe their eyes, but they wasted no time before they got him back on board, and Erik wasted no time before he told them what he and Sven the Strong had discovered.

'But how are we to get Golden Dragon onto that lake beneath the sea?' asked Ragnar Forkbeard.

'The same way that Sven the Strong and I got there,' replied Erik. 'We must take Golden Dragon herself over the Edge of the World and through the Waterfall of Seas!'

As soon as Erik had said this, a great debate broke out. Some said it was impossible, while some said it was madness. Some said it might work while some said it wouldn't, but at length Erik called them all to be quiet.

'We have no choice!' he said, and he began to organise the fearful task, securing both

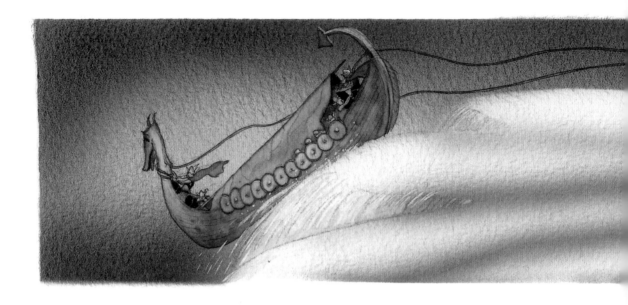

prow and stern of Golden Dragon to the rock with all the rope they had. Then they laid the mast along her and threw the sail over it like a tent. 'That may keep some of the water out,' said Erik, 'for if Golden Dragon were to fill up with water, I doubt whether these ropes could support her weight.'

Then, with many a fearful prayer to the gods of sea and boats and men, they began to pay out the ropes that held Golden Dragon to the rock.

'But remember!' Erik shouted, above the roaring waters, 'Do not look into the abyss! We shall need all our strength to hold onto our ship!'

And so Erik and his men let their ship Golden Dragon be dragged through the mist and spray until they came out of it and hung there on the Edge of the World. And the waters raged and pulled at their ship, and the timbers creaked and the ropes sighed, and the men hung onto them with all their might.

'We must look over the Edge of the World,' they murmured one to the other. 'It would be a crime to come so far and not to see such a wonderful thing …' But even as they murmured they heard Erik's voice: 'Let go of the ropes!' And at his command Golden Dragon shot out from the Edge of the World, hurled by the force of the waters, and seemed to hang in mid-air over the great abyss, before the ropes went taut and the ship went crashing back into the wall of falling water. And there was not one man amongst them, who then had time to so much as think of looking over the side and down into the abyss.

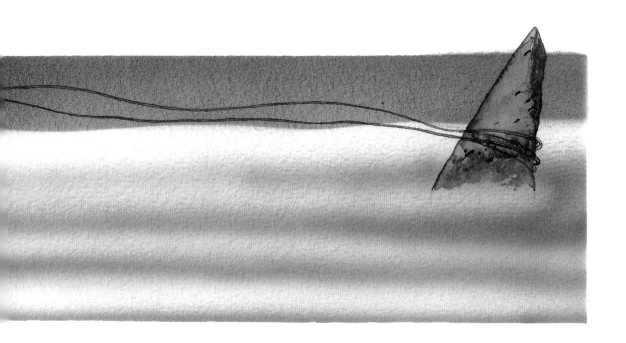

As the ship hit the wall of water, there was a dreadful crack, which they all heard even above the deafening roar, and they all knew what it meant … one rope had snapped. Golden Dragon lurched and the men were hurled to one end as the water ripped under the covering sail and smashed through the boat, sending oars, and shields and provisions flying. And for a moment Golden Dragon seemed to dangle there in the full force of the deluge, and the men clung on for dear life, knowing neither where they were nor what was happening. And then suddenly the ship swung again, as if kicked by the water, and they were in darkness, and the noise abated. And they opened their eyes, and found they were lying on their side in the caverns beneath the Edge of the World, with Sven the Strong laughing at their frightened faces …

THE SECRET LAKE

1. THE FOURTEENTH ORB

WHEN THEY HAD RECOVERED from their desperate plunge through the Waterfall of Seas, Erik and his men dragged their ship, Golden Dragon, through the cavern beneath the Edge of the World, to the Secret Lake that Erik and Sven the Strong had discovered. They lit the few torches that they had managed to keep dry, and set off to explore that nether world of darkness and echoes.

Erik and his men shivered, as their ship slid on under a sky of stone. And the splashing of their oars was echoed in a thousand caves and passages and came back like laughter.

All at once, they saw a light glowing in the water beneath them – deep in the lake.

'What can it be?' they wondered, as the light grew bigger and brighter, until the whole of the Secret Lake was shining with it. And then they gasped in amazement, for by the brightness of that light they could now see the roof of the cavern above them was not just bare rock, but was covered in wonderful patterns of blue and gold and silver.

Then Ragnar Forkbeard shouted out, 'Look!' And they all looked into the bright lake and saw a dark shape rising up from the depths. 'Is it some terrible monster of the deep?' asked Erik's men one to the other.

But before they had time to be afraid, the thing had bobbed up onto the surface, and they could see it was not a monster of the deep. It was like a huge orange. And it sat there floating on the water.

Erik and his men rowed right round it, but they could make nothing of it. It was simply a perfectly smooth orange ball, twice as high as the mainmast of Golden Dragon.

Erik turned to Thorkhild and said, 'Have you ever seen such a thing?' But Thorkhild shook his head. Then Ragnar Forkbeard reached out his hand and touched it.

'It is quite warm,' he said. 'This is something I have never seen before nor even heard tell of.'

Then some of Erik's men were filled with fear. 'We don't know what it is nor what it may do to us …' they said. 'Let us attack it and send it back down to the bottom of this lake from whence it came.'

But Erik said, 'It has done us no harm. Let us leave it in peace, since we can find out nothing more about it.'

But even before Erik had finished speaking there was a fearful CRACK! that echoed over the lake, and Erik and his men threw themselves to the deck. Then there was another loud CRACK! and another. Then silence. Erik looked up and saw the great orange globe opening up like a four-petalled flower, and there in the centre sat the strangest creature. It was all spiky and knobbly, but it had a great smile on its face, and it said, 'Follow me!'

Then it got astride a golden fish, and Erik and his men rowed after it in Golden Dragon. They travelled like this for several miles across the glowing lake, deep into the painted cave. At last the creature stopped and pointed to an island in the middle of the lake.

'Go to the island,' said the creature. 'You will find my master there,' and it turned the golden fish around and started back.

But Erik said, 'Wait! Before you go, won't you tell us who or what you are?'

But the knobbly creature just grinned and said, 'Ha! I like that! You mean to say you don't recognise me?'

'I'm sorry,' replied Erik, 'but I've never seen you before in my life.' And the others shook their heads in agreement.

'But you all made me what I am!' it said. 'Didn't you know?'

'I don't understand,' said Erik.

'Deary me!' said the creature. 'Where are you lot from? Do you mean to say you didn't know that that was the Fourteenth Orb?'

'What's that?' they asked.

'Well, the Fourteenth Orb is different from the rest,' said the creature.

'The rest?' asked Thorkhild.

'The rest of the twenty-six. Don't you even know about them?'

Erik and the others shook their heads and the creature looked at them in amazement and said, 'Kobold put them in the lake …'

'Who is Kob …' began Thorkhild but Erik kicked his shin and the knobbly creature went on, 'Some of the orbs are to keep out foes. Some of them are to welcome friends. But the Fourteenth Orb is different from all the rest. Whatever comes out of it is just like whoever finds it. If they attack it, a terrible monster leaps out and attacks them … If they are friendly, a friendly creature shows them the way. You were a bit of a mixture, which is why I'm like I am: knobbly but friendly.'

'I see,' said Erik. 'But one final question: who is Kobold?'

At this the creature burst into laughter and the caves echoed all around. 'You'd better ask Kobold that!' it said, and it sped off back across the lake on its golden fish.

Erik and his men looked at each other, and then made their way to the island that stood in the middle of the shining lake. As they landed, they heard a tapping noise, and found a short man in dirty leather breeches at the bottom of a hole he was digging.

'My goodness me!' he said. 'Visitors! I wasn't expecting any visitors for at least another three thousand years!'

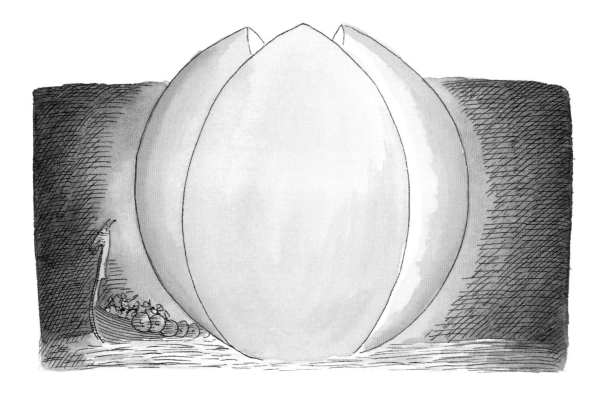

'We are looking for the master of the Secret Lake, whose name is Kobold,' said Erik. 'Can you take us to him?'

'Well, fancy that!' exclaimed the little man. 'Imagine going to all that trouble just to visit old Kobold!'

So Erik explained who they were and how they had come there and how they wished to return to the world above to continue their quest. And the little man nodded and nodded until you'd think his head would have fallen off. Then he said, 'Well! How d'you do! How d'you do! I am Kobold. I made all this …' and he pointed round at the painted cavern and the bright lake.

'But it's a weary time now,' he said. 'Look at this hole. Not much of a hole and yet I've been at it for six hundred years now. I think I've lost my touch. Why, when I built this whole cavern, it only took me a week and six minutes to paint it! Ah, those were the days,' and he leant sadly on this spade.

'But can you tell us how to get out of here, Kobold?' asked Erik. And Kobold looked at Erik out of the corner of his eye and said, 'Get out of here? Why? Don't you like my cavern?'

'Well … yes …' said Erik, 'but we must get on with our quest.'

'All in good time,' said the little man, 'all in good time. Let's eat first.'

And he led the way up a small hill in the middle of the island and disappeared down a hole in the top. And Erik and the others followed after.

They found themselves going down and down through winding passageways, and all the time the little man in leather breeches skipped and hopped in front of them. Eventually they came out in a vast hall, the floor, the walls, and the ceiling of which were lacquered with shining blue enamel. A long table was set out in the middle, laid out with all the good things to eat you could think of. And pretty soon they had all fallen to it, for they had not eaten for many days.

When they had finished, Erik turned to the little man and said, 'Kobold, show us the way out.'

'All in good time,' replied Kobold. 'First you need to rest,' and he opened up a trap-door in the floor and led them all down a flight of sky-blue stairs into an azure chamber laid out with beds. There they slept as soundly as they had ever slept anywhere.

How long they slept, none of them knew, for there was no sun to rise in that underworld. But when they awoke, Erik once more found Kobold and asked him once more to show them the way out. But Kobold replied, 'Today is a very special day! It is my birthday! Won't you do me the honour of attending a banquet tonight in celebration?' And they could not refuse.

The next day Kobold was too ill to show them the way out. And the day after that he had some urgent business to do. And the day after that there was another reason, and so on the next day, and the next day.

And so time slipped by in Kobold's cave. Until at length Erik went to Kobold as he sat in the little hole he had been digging for six hundred years and said, 'Kobold! You sit there pretending to dig your hole. But you are still no deeper than you were when we first met you, or than you were six hundred years ago. And I know why.'

'Why?' asked Kobold. 'Tell me and I shall show you the way out at once.'

'The reason you cannot finish digging that hole, Kobold,' replied Erik, 'is that you don't want to. You have spent your life making this palace underground, and you know that if you ever finish it, you will have nothing else to do … no purpose …'

A dirty tear formed in Kobold's left eye and he sighed and said, 'You are right.'

'But we do have a purpose, Kobold,' said Erik. 'We seek the land where the sun goes at night.'

'Why?' asked Kobold.

'Because I once swore I would never sleep in my bed again until I had sought it.'

'That doesn't seem a very good reason to me,' said Kobold.

'Well, we're not asking you,' said Erik. 'Just show us the way out of here, will you?'

And then Kobold looked even sadder than ever, and a dirty tear formed in his right eye and rolled down his cheek, and he said, 'I can't.'

'What!' shouted Erik. 'But you built all this and dug out these caverns and passageways, didn't you?'

'Yes,' said Kobold, 'I did, but to tell the truth I did it all so long ago … so long ago that … I have forgotten how to get out myself. Although heaven knows, how much I'd like to sometimes.' And with that great dirty tears started running down his cheeks from both eyes at once, and he sat down in his hole.

'Then come with us, Kobold,' said Erik, 'for we shall not rest until we have found the way out.'

'Thank you … thank you …' replied Kobold, 'let me think about it for a few hundred years, will you?'

'I'm sorry,' said Erik, 'we are mere men. We do not have as long as you on this earth nor under it, and we must do what we must do now, or it will be too late.'

'But just stop a little longer,' pleaded Kobold, 'and consider what else you might be doing instead …'

'I'm sorry,' replied Erik, 'life is too short. Goodbye, Kobold!' And with that he and his men got back on board Golden Dragon, and were soon paddling across the Secret Lake into the Unknown …

2. VIPER RAIN

THEY HADN'T GONE FAR before Ragnar Forkbeard pointed up at the painted roof of the cavern and said, 'How strange! The patterns are moving …' And sure enough, as everyone looked they saw the bright lines of colour were weaving in and out of each other in ceaseless turmoil.

'What can this mean?' murmured Erik. But even as he spoke some of the lines of colour began to peel away from the rest and dropped down into the shining lake, and there was a hiss like steam as they hit the water. And as the men watched in amazement, a thin line of blue came away from the roof directly above Golden Dragon and fell onto the deck, writhing and turning.

'Don't touch it!' cried Sven the Strong. 'Don't you see? It's a snake!'

And at that moment writhing lines of every colour began to fall thick and fast, until the shining lake was boiling and the deck of Golden Dragon was covered with coiling snakes.

Erik and his men ran here and there, knocking them back into the waters or cutting off their heads. But there were so many, and they were so quick that many of the men were bitten in the heel, and many of the men were bitten in the leg, and they lay still on the deck where they had been bitten.

Then a red viper with gold crosses on its back fell onto Ragnar Forkbeard's shoulder and, before Erik could strike it off, it had bitten Ragnar in the neck and he fell where he stood.

Erik called out to Thorkhild, 'Help me, Thorkhild!' and the two of them together struggled with the mast and laid it from stem to stern, and threw the sail over it as a roof to keep off the viper rain. Then they were able to clear the decks, and tend to those who had been bitten.

'Ragnar Forkbeard,' whispered Erik, 'do you still breathe?' Ragnar Forkbeard opened his eyes and said, 'Let us turn back, Erik. For we shall never find our way out of these caves …'

At these words they all fell silent, and they heard the hissing of the viper rain in the water

of the lake, and the thudding of the snakes landing on their canvas roof. And then a strange thing happened. One by one each of Erik's men who had been bitten opened his eyes, and each began to say the same thing, 'Let us turn back, Erik. For we shall never find our way out of these caves …'

'And besides,' said Ragnar Forkbeard, 'why should we ever want to leave? It is beautiful here and we are safe …'

Erik frowned, and did not reply. But Sven the Strong was already on his feet, shouting, 'You are mad! Of course we can find our way out from these caves!' But Ragnar Forkbeard and the others were on their feet too, and they had drawn their swords.

'It is you who are mad!' they cried. 'Can't you see how beautiful it is here? This is what we have been searching for! This is the goal of our quest!'

And so saying they raised their swords and began to advance on Erik and the rest. Whereupon Erik held up his hand and said, 'Ragnar Forkbeard! You are right! It is beautiful here! Let us stay forever!'

Sven the Strong looked at Erik in amazement, but before he could reply, Thorkhild cried out, 'Look!' and they all turned and saw that the viper rain had ceased, and as they watched, a rainbow of snakes formed over the lake and Golden Dragon glided through it.

3. THE MERMAID'S GARDEN

AS THEY CAME OUT the other side of the snake-rainbow, they suddenly saw the wall of the cavern open up like the doors of a great castle, to reveal a dazzling cave of ruby red and emerald green, and there inside, to their astonishment, they saw Kobold. He was no longer streaked with soil and sweat or dressed in dirty leather breeches, but he was sitting on a throne of gold and silver and he wore a crown that sparkled with the fires of every gem that can be dug out of the earth.

'I am so glad you've decided to stay with me in my Kingdom!' said Kobold, and he clapped his hands and a hundred mermaids formed a circle around Golden Dragon and swayed this way and that while they sang a strange song … a song of things of long, long ago … things half-remembered … things that happened before men knew they were men … before the time when the seas were home … and Erik and his men grew drowsy and fell asleep, one by one, while the mermaids' song echoed in the thousand caves across the Secret Lake.

When Erik awoke, he found himself and his companions lying naked on the shore of the lake.

'What has happened to us?' asked a voice, and Erik turned to find Thorkhild at his elbow.

'I'm not sure,' whispered Erik. 'But one thing I do know – we must find the antidote to the venom that now courses in the veins of Ragnar Forkbeard and the others, and that has not killed them but has taken away from them their will to go on.

Otherwise, I fear we shall never leave these caves and caverns.'

So Erik and Thorkhild crept up to a mermaid who was sitting on the pile of all their clothes combing her hair, and softly Erik put his hand over her mouth to stop her singing, and held her arms to stop her combing her hair, and whispered in her ear, 'Don't be afraid, sea-maiden. We are only travellers passing through.' The mermaid dropped her comb and replied:

'If you are but travellers passing through,
I'll help you as I'm bound to do.'

Then she turned her eyes to look at Erik, and he thought she had the most beautiful face he had ever seen.

But he looked away from her and said, 'Where is the antidote to the viper's venom?'

And the mermaid smiled, and her eyes sparkled, and her voice was so soft and so gentle and so nearly a song that Erik felt his resolve draining out through his toes into the sea.

'You must come with me,' she said, 'to my garden, where a herb grows that only human hands can pick. That is the antidote you seek.'

'Don't go!' whispered Thorkhild, 'For I mistrust this mermaid, and it is fraught with danger to go where she lives ... at the bottom of the lake.'

'I shall not look at her,' replied Erik. 'And I shall not listen to her. I shall only pick the herb and return.'

'Come!' said the mermaid, switching her fishy tail. 'You need not look at me, and I shall not speak once we are in the water, but hold my hand and I shall guide you safely down.'

So Erik took the mermaid's hand, and together they dived into the bright lake, and she gave a flick of her fish's tail and they sped down and down faster than a stone sinks.

It was much deeper than Erik could ever have imagined, and it got saltier and colder, the deeper they went. Down and down until all at once Erik saw the bottom below him, and there was a grand palace built out of giant shells, and all around the palace were pleasant gardens, with seaweed lawns and huge sea-anemone trees. Hand in hand Erik and the mermaid passed through an arbour of sea-wrack, into a plot where rockweed and sea moss, kelp and sargassum grew in neat rows. And all the time Erik did not look at the mermaid,

and all the time she spoke not one word. At last, however, she pointed to a small herb that grew by the edge, and Erik reached out his hand and picked what he could, and all the time the mermaid held onto his other hand tight.

Then Erik knew he had to return to the surface, for he had no breath left in his body. But when he tried to pull his hand away, he found he could not. The mermaid would not let go, but held onto his hand tighter than ever. Erik was bursting for breath, so he turned to the mermaid to show her his plight, but as he did so, his heart filled with horror, for he found himself holding not the hand of the mermaid, but the hand of the Old Man of the Sea.

'Ha! Ha!' cried the Old Man of the Sea. 'You out-tricked me once! But you shan't again!' And he held onto Erik's hand and squeezed it till it hurt.

But as he did so a voice said, 'You are mistaken, Old Man of the Sea! It was I who out-tricked you last time and I who shall out-trick you again!' They both turned to see Thorkhild as he wound a piece of seaweed round the Old Man's eyes, and as the Old Man of the Sea put his hands to his eyes, Erik pulled free his hand, and in that moment Erik and Thorkhild made their escape.

Up and up they swam, and they could hear the Old Man of the Sea coming after them, and they could hear his angry shouts. But up they went and reached the shore just as the Old Man of the Sea's hand came up out of the water and grabbed at Thorkhild's leg. But Erik seized Blueblade, his sword, which was lying on the shore and struck off the Old Man of the Sea's hand. And the Old Man of the Sea disappeared back into the shining lake with a howl of rage and pain.

Then Erik asked Thorkhild what had made him follow, and Thorkhild replied, 'After you'd gone, I picked up the mermaid's comb, which she had dropped, and I knew it was no mermaid's comb, for its teeth were the bones of human fingers, so I followed you down and saw her change into the Old Man of the Sea.'

'And lucky we are that she did!' cried Erik.

'What do you mean?' asked Thorkhild. 'You all but drowned.'

'But also,' replied Erik, 'we now know, since the Old Man of the Sea lives in this lake, that it must lead us back to the open sea.'

So there and then they gave the antidote to Ragnar Forkbeard and the other men who had been bitten in the viper rain. Then they all dressed as quickly as they could.

And though they heard the mermaids singing behind them, and Kobold shouting after them, they rowed Golden Dragon over the Secret Lake, through the painted cavern and down a thousand twisting passageways. They dragged their ship through rock-filled chambers, and hauled her up subterranean cascades, until at long last they suddenly found themselves sailing out onto the open sea once more, with the clear sky above them.

THE GIANT'S HARP

THE SUN SHONE DOWN, and Golden Dragon sped through the blue seas until they came to a land of palm trees. Here they made a camp to rest and collect fresh water and food.

One day, Erik and his men heard music coming from far away, borne upon the breeze. 'Who can be playing such music?' they asked one another. 'Let us go and find out.'

But Erik said, 'No. We must finish our business here and then leave, for we still have far to go.' And so they continued to work, gathering fruits and searching for fresh water.

Some days passed, however, and still they had not discovered fresh water in that land for, although there were dates and coconuts and other fruits, there were no rivers or even streams that they could see. Erik and Ulf Sigfusson were searching in a rocky ravine, when once again they heard the beautiful music.

'Surely,' said Erik, 'whoever it is that plays such music must themselves be beautiful beyond belief …'

'Let us see for ourselves,' said Ulf Sigfusson.

'The sound is certainly not far away,' said Erik. 'And who knows, it may lead us to the water that we seek.'

So Erik and Ulf Sigfusson began to follow the sound of the beautiful music.

They followed it through the ravine, and the great cliffs of rock towered up high on either side of them. And still the sound led them on, although the way got steep and the path became rockier and harder.

Suddenly they found their way blocked by a fearsome giant, three times as tall as a man, with silver skin and hair that reached right down to the ground.

'At last I've caught you!' cried the giant. 'You're the ones who have been stealing my sheep, eh? Well, I'll teach you, I'll roast you over my fire tonight, and eat you just as you have eaten my sheep!'

'We have not been stealing your sheep!' cried Erik. 'We are only looking to see who makes such beautiful music!'

'What music?' roared the giant.

'The music that you hear borne so gently on the breeze,' replied Ulf Sigfusson.

'I hear no music!' roared the giant. 'There is no music!' And he threw a net over the two companions and dragged them to his cave.

The cave was dark and smelt of blood, and yet the strange thing was that in it they could hear music louder than ever.

'Listen, giant!' cried Erik. 'Surely you can hear that beautiful music now!'

'I hear no music,' replied the giant. 'There is no music.' And with that he threw them into a corner and went to fetch some kindling for his fire.

While he was gone, Erik and Ulf Sigfusson got out their knives and started to cut their way out of the net. But they found that their knives simply would not cut it – no matter what they did.

'Now we are lost!' cried Erik, 'for I hear the tread of the giant's feet returning with the wood for his fire, so he can roast us for his dinner tonight!'

But Ulf Sigfusson replied, 'Listen to the music! It is more beautiful than ever!'

'Never mind about that!' cried Erik. 'We must get free of this net before the giant returns, or we shall never listen to any music ever again!'

But it was too late. A dark shadow blotted out the light from the entrance of the cave, as the giant returned, and began to light his fire.

'Listen, giant!' cried Erik. 'Surely you hear that music now! Its beauty surpasses anything I have ever heard before.'

But the giant just grunted and said, 'I hear no music! There is no music!' Then he went out to sharpen his axe to chop off their heads.

'Quick!' said Erik to Ulf Sigfusson, 'Do as I say!' But Ulf Sigfusson was so enraptured by the music that he could hear nothing else. And even though Erik shook him and slapped him, he was as a man in a dream. And outside they could hear the sound of an axe being sharpened.

Then Erik put his arms round his comrade and rolled with him in the net towards the fire. When they got near enough, Erik poked his hand through the net and seized a burning branch, and set fire to the net. The net burst into flames, and Erik and Ulf Sigfusson leapt out before they could be burnt themselves.

But even as they did so, they heard the heavy tread of the giant outside.

'Quick!' cried Erik, but Ulf Sigfusson was not listening. He was walking back into the cave like a man in a dream.

'Ulf!' cried Erik. 'What are you doing?'

'The music is coming from deep within this very cave,' replied Ulf.

'But the giant is returning with his sharp axe!' cried Erik. 'We must go now or we shall be caught!'

But Ulf Sigfusson was not listening, and before Erik could say or do anything else, he heard the tread of the giant's foot at the entrance of the cave, and he turned and saw the giant entering the cave with his newly sharpened axe. So without waiting another second, Erik ran after his comrade, deeper into the giant's cave.

They picked their way down a narrow twisting passageway, lit only by the burning branch that Erik still carried. And after a short time they heard a dreadful roar behind them, as the giant found the burnt-up net and realised he had been cheated out of his dinner.

As Erik and Ulf Sigfusson made their way deeper and deeper into the giant's cave, the music got louder and louder, and even Erik began to be caught in the spell of its beauty. But he stripped some bark from the burning branch and stuffed it into his ears so that he could not hear.

'Surely,' said Ulf Sigfusson, 'it is a god who makes such sounds!'

And then they turned a corner and saw the most extraordinary sight. There was the musician playing a harp that was painted with magic signs. But the musician was not a god, nor was the musician beautiful as they had imagined. In fact the musician was neither man nor woman nor child … It was the wind that blew through the tunnels and passageways of the giant's cave. And the harp was hanging there in the midst of a great cavern, and all around it, Erik could see by the flickering light of his burning branch dim shapes … hundreds and thousands of them. And as Erik peered into the gloom he could see that there were men and women, birds and beasts all gathered around that wonderful harp, each and every one of them gazing up at it … without moving … without blinking an eye … and each and every one of them was gaunt and thin and grey as the rock of the cave. And Erik knew that many of them had been sitting there in that darkness for thousands of years, under the enchantment of the magic harp, for they were wraiths – the ghosts of living creatures about to die but who could not because their very souls had become enchanted by the music and could not leave.

There were bears and eagles, dogs and cats, lizards and bats and even the giant's sheep, all sitting there transfixed. And then Erik noticed Ulf Sigfusson, falling to his knees, his eyes, too, fixed on that harp, and Erik knew that Ulf was under the spell completely and that he himself would have fallen long ago but for the plugs of bark in his ears. But even so, Erik could feel his will ebbing, as the notes of the harp made themselves heard even to him and he felt an uncontrollable urge to take the plugs of bark out of his ears so that he might hear the music better. But he did not. Instead he strode through that enchanted throng of wraiths. Then he reached out his

hand to the harp and took hold of it … and, as he did so, its strings vibrated along the bones of his arm and entered his mind so that he heard them as clear as if he had heard them with his ears. Their beauty wrapped around his soul like a shroud, and he felt his soul begin to slumber, and his body weaken, and he too found himself falling to his knees.

But even as he fell he kept his hold upon the harp, so that he tore it down from the peg on which it hung … All but one of the strings broke, and he held the harp on the ground where the winds could not reach it, and the music stopped.

The moment it stopped a strange groan rose up from the throng of shadows, and every one of them turned to look at Erik, and their eyes were tiny points of white light, and their mouths cracked open, and their white teeth shone sharp, like a million daggers in the night, and the groan turned into a roar of rage.

Without another moment's thought, Erik leapt to his feet, and, still clutching the harp, he ran as hard as he could back the way he had come, back up the passageway, and Ulf

Sigfusson followed. Behind them they heard the fearful noise as all those tortured creatures from the past clamoured with rage and disappointment and began to fly after them.

Erik and Ulf Sigfusson ran with every ounce of strength in their bodies, and yet, even so, those creatures gained on them inch by inch.

'We cannot make it!' cried Ulf Sigfusson.

'Keep running!' shouted Erik.

And suddenly there they were back in the giant's cave, and the giant himself was blocking their way.

'So there you are!' he cried, and he raised his newly sharpened axe.

'Wait!' cried Erik, 'we did not steal your sheep! It was this that stole them!' And he lifted up the harp, and the wind plucked a note from the last unbroken string.

And the giant dropped his axe and his eyes went wide with wonder. 'My harp!' he cried, and he snatched it from Erik's hand.

But even as he did so the furious wraiths burst into the giant's cave, their eyes white and their teeth bared and the cry of blood rising from their throats – both man and beast alike. And there and then they would have torn Erik and Ulf Sigfusson to pieces, had not a strange thing happened. The giant was holding the harp in his fingers, and it looked like a child's toy in his huge hand, but he plucked the last unbroken string, and a high clear note echoed round and round the cave, and disappeared down the myriad passageways and retuned deeper and higher in a magical chord … A hush fell over all that ghastly throng, and each and every one of them heaved a great sigh, and as Erik and Ulf Sigfusson watched, their souls rose up from their bodies and flew out of the door of the cave to go to wherever spirits go.

Then the giant turned to the two comrades, and now he no longer seemed a terrible ogre.

'This is my harp,' he said. 'On it I played such music that everyone who heard it was my friend. But the Witch of the Wind grew jealous – for she wanders lonely through the world, never standing still, always moving from place to place. She stole my harp to ensnare the souls of men and beasts, and since then I have dragged out my days in solitude here, for no living thing would stay with me.'

'But why did you not hear it?' asked Erik.

'Ah,' said the giant, 'that is my one great sadness … I alone cannot hear the music of my own harp.'

Then the giant asked Erik and Ulf Sigfusson what they would like as a reward, and they told him of their search for water.

'Go down to the ravine where you first heard the music,' said the giant, 'and you will find what you seek under the old cedar tree that grows there.'

So Erik and Ulf Sigfusson thanked the giant and hurried to the ravine. But under the old cedar tree they found neither stream nor well nor pond, only a jug with a crack in it.

'The giant is playing tricks with us,' said Ulf Sigfusson. But Erik lifted the jug up and said: 'In a way he has told the truth, for look, the jug is full of water!' and Erik tasted the water and found that it was good water.

'But what is one jug amongst so many of us?' asked Ulf Sigfusson.

'Perhaps he did not realise there were more of us,' said Erik.

So the companions returned to the giant's cave and explained how many of them there were. Then the giant took the jug and – to their astonishment – he emptied it out on the ground and then handed it back.

'What sort of an answer is this?' asked Erik, but no sooner had he said the words then he looked into the jug, and found that it was once again full of water. And when he emptied it, he found that it refilled itself.

Then Erik and Ulf Sigfusson returned to Golden Dragon, and after that they never went short of water again.

HOW DEATH CHALLENGED ERiK

O**HE NIGHT ERIK AND HIS MEN** were sleeping in their ship, when they heard a strange noise. Each and every one of them woke up with a start, and then lay listening in the blackness, while the waves tossed them up and down.

'What is that noise?' asked Ragnar Forkbeard. 'It sounds like a deep drum, drumming across the sea!'

'No,' said Sven the Strong. 'It sounds like a great bell, tolling across the sea.'

'Ssh!' said Thorkhild, and they all listened, and as they listened the drum and the bell seemed to beat in time with each other, and then they felt a cold breeze blow across their faces.

'It is getting closer,' said Erik, 'whatever it is.'

Then they all strained their eyes, and peered into the black night.

'Look!' whispered Ragnar Forkbeard. 'There is a light!' And sure enough, far, far away, somewhere between the black water and the black sky, a dim lantern was swinging towards them.

'Who can it be in these uncharted waters?' they asked one another. 'Surely no other men have travelled this far?'

But as they wondered, the lantern swung closer, and they could see it reflected a thousand times on the always-changing edges of the water. And as the drum beat louder and the bell tolled stronger, they began to see dim figures and more carrying lanterns behind.

'Why!' cried Sven the Strong. 'What sort of men are these that venture without a boat amongst the tossing waves, and tread a path across the sea as if it were the broad highway?'

And sure enough, Erik and his men watched in wonder as the strange column filed past Golden Dragon, six abreast, their lanterns swinging and glimmering feebly as they marched.

'It is the March of the Dead,' murmured Thorkhild.

Just then a rider on a horse galloped up, and the horse reared and stamped its hooves on the sea, sending the salt spray flying. And all the while, the dead filed past. The rider wore a hood, but inside the hood they could see a skull's eyes looking at them.

'Are you Death?' asked Thorkhild.

But the horse reared up and whinnied, and the waves crashed around them and, if the figure replied, they could not hear it.

'Have you come for all of us?' asked Erik. 'Or for but one of us?'

Again the horse snorted and pawed the sea, and the waves smashed so hard together that you could not have heard a huntsman's horn six inches from your ear, and, if the figure replied, none of them heard it. And all the while the dead filed past, and their dingy lanterns swung over the black sea.

'Speak to us!' cried Sven the Strong. 'Tell us what you want, or else leave us alone!'

At that a shout – or perhaps it was a laugh – went up from all the dead as they filed past, and the rider on the horse pointed a bony finger at Sven the Strong.

'Spare his life!' cried Erik. 'It is I who brought us all on this venture – take me if you must take one of us now!'

The rider turned his hollow eyes on Erik, and spoke. And at every word the lanterns all went out, and flickered on again only in the spaces between his words.

'I am Death,' said the figure. 'And none of you shall cheat me. I will take you all. And I will take you when I choose … But enjoy a game now and then, and if you will play me at chess, I will spare your friend's life for now.'

'I will play you at chess!' cried Erik.

'Don't!' whispered Thorkhild.

'Very good,' said Death. 'You will know me when you see me!'

And with that he rode off, and the last of the dead filed off into the black night.

Dawn was breaking, and Erik and his men stretched and yawned, and wondered if they had dreamt it all. But Thorkhild took Erik on one side, and said: 'You must not play chess with Death. You can only lose.'

'We shall see,' said Erik, and the wind blew them to a green shore.

THE LAND WHERE THE SUN GOES AT NIGHT

WHEN ERIK AND HIS MEN landed on that green shore, they looked around in wonder.

'What if this were the land we have been seeking all this while?' they whispered one to the other.

'It is indeed a fair country,' murmured Ragnar Forkbeard. 'See how green the grass is.'

'There is wild game in the forests!' reported a search party.

'There are sheep and cattle in the meadows,' reported another.

'And fruit and water and trees for timber – everything men could need!' reported yet another.

'I have heard my father tell, many a time and oft,' murmured Erik, 'that the land where the sun goes at night is such a place as this …'

'Can it be that we are truly there at last?' asked Ragnar Forkbeard, but even as he spoke, they heard shouting and running feet, and they looked up and saw Sven the Strong running down the hillside towards the beach.

'Get your arms!' he cried.

'What is it?' asked Erik, but Sven the Strong shook his head.

'Even if I were to tell you what I have found, you would not believe me,' he said, 'Come and see for yourselves – but bring every weapon you have, for you will need them.'

And so they armed themselves, and went with Sven the Strong back up the hill. They walked on for some time, wondering what it could be, but no matter how many times they asked Sven what it was, he shook his head and refused to answer at all.

After some while they reached a high plateau, and found themselves looking down into a fertile plain. There were fields and meadows, sheep on the hills, a village in the distance, and through it all ran a broad river, sparkling in the sun.

'Look over there,' whispered Sven the Strong, and as Erik and the others watched, they saw a strange, hunched figure go into a field and start to sow corn.

'I only see a farmer sowing corn,' said Erik. 'He has a hunched back, but there is nothing so extraordinary about that.'

'Watch,' whispered Sven the Strong, and as he spoke, the hunchbacked farmer finished sowing the field, and the moment the last seed was sown a most extraordinary thing happened. As Erik and his comrades watched, green shoots began to thrust out from the earth, and the corn began to grow, and before even a word of surprise could come to their lips, the field was full of ripe corn, and the hunchbacked farmer had begun to reap it.

'Now I truly believe we have found what we sought,' said Erik, 'for I have heard my father many a time describe such a place as this as the land where the sun goes at night … a land so fertile that no one need ever go hungry again.'

But no sooner had he said these words, than there was a roar, and Erik and his men turned to see a terrible creature glaring down at them. It was as tall as an oak tree, and its head was in the middle of its chest. Before they had time to raise their bows, the creature gave another roar, and as it opened its mouth they could see its teeth had been filed to sharp points.

'Now I see why we have brought our weapons!' cried Ragnar Forkbeard, and he raised his bow just as the creature took another step towards them, and it stretched out its arm so that its clenched fist hung above them, blotting out the sun.

'Our swords and arrows will be but pins and penknives against such a creature!' cried Thorkhild, but Sven the Strong had already let fly an arrow, and it flew straight and true, and pierced the terrible creature in the left eye. Whereupon the creature roared in pain, fell to its knees, and its fist came crashing down amongst the companions, like the bough of some mighty oak. And two of them were crushed under its weight, and screamed out in agony. Then Thorkhild let fly his arrow, and it flew straight and true, and pierced the monster in the right eye, and again the monster roared out in pain, and toppled forwards, and smashed down like some great tree, and the ground shook. As it fell, the companions ran for their lives, and the fist that it had held above them opened, and out rolled a huge piece of gold shaped like the crescent moon.

'This is more wonderful than ever!' murmured Erik, and was about to rush forward to seize the precious metal, when he stopped, and looked down upon the plain below them. There he saw more mis-shapen creatures running towards the plateau where they stood.

'Quick!' shouted Erik, above the roaring of the wounded monster. 'We must return to Golden Dragon as fast as ever we can, for we will soon be outnumbered!' Then Ragnar Forkbeard seized the golden moon – though it was all he could do to lift it up – and they all turned to retrace their steps. But even as they turned, the blood froze in their veins, for there – standing in the path by which they had come – were twenty … thirty … maybe fifty of the creatures, each as tall and as mis-shapen as the first, and each began to roar and began to stride towards Erik and his men.

'Follow me!' cried Erik, and without another word they began scrambling and running up the mountain.

Up they climbed – up and up – and behind them they heard the monstrous beings roaring for their wounded comrade. But still Erik and his men climbed until, just as the sun was setting, they stopped, and, looking down, they saw the monsters turning and going back down the mountainside.

'They have gone to gather more of their kind,' said Erik.

'What are we to do?' his men began to whisper to each other. 'We have found at last

the land where the sun goes at night, and yet here we are trapped on this mountainside, cut off from our ship, without food or drink, while this monstrous enemy surrounds us, and gathers its forces to finish us off once and for all.'

'It is indeed hard to be near and yet so far,' murmured Thorkhild. But just then a strange and even more wonderful thing began to happen: the mountainside began to tremble, and began belching out smoke so that Erik and his men were forced back down the rock face for some way. They stood there dumbfounded, and trembling with fear, as the very earth shook, and the smoke billowed out and formed a black cloud that hung over the mountain. Then there was a terrible C-R-A-C-K! and the summit of the mountain split apart, and a sheet of flame shot out into the air.

'We are doomed!' cried Erik's men. 'There are monsters below us and a volcano above! This surely is the end!'

But there was one among them who was not white with fear and who did not tremble. Thorkhild was standing, wide-eyed in wonder, staring into the sheet of flame at the top of the mountain.

'What is it, Thorkhild?' cried Erik. 'What do you see?'

'I see something I never thought to see again,' replied Thorkhild, and he began to walk towards the flames that lit up the gathering night.

'Come back!' cried Ragnar Forkbeard.

'What are you doing?' cried Sven the Strong.

But Thorkhild was climbing up as if in a trance, and, as he did so, the black cloud descended upon him, and he vanished from their sight.

As soon as he was gone, the mountain ceased shaking, and the noise of thunder, which had filled their ears, abated. Erik's men looked at one another, and each one wondered what it was that Thorkhild had seen.

'What was it?' they asked Erik, but Erik only shook his head and replied, 'Wait … we shall soon see for ourselves.'

Then the smoke began to lift, and as it did so they all gasped. For there stood Thorkhild at the very summit of the mountain. He was blackened from head to toe, and his eyes were white – as if the heat of the flame had seared them of sight, and they knew that he was blind. Yet he was smiling, and in his hand he held a sword that was glowing like all the stars in heaven, and each and every one of the companions gasped, for they recognised it at once.

'The Starsword!' cried Thorkhild. 'And I thought I should never see it nor hold it in my hands again. But now I can feel its power coursing through my arms, and my whole body. It is the Starsword … my hands know it, and in my blindness I see it as bright and shining as that day when it slew the Dogfighters on that beach so far away and so long ago!'

'It is the Starsword!' cried Erik, 'and it saved us then, and it shall save us now! For I believe there is no enemy in this world that can withstand that magic blade.'

And even as he was speaking, they heard a roar, and they looked down, and saw myriad torches on the mountainside below them burning in the dark, and swarming up the scree towards them …

THE LAND WHERE THE SUN GOES AT NIGHT

'Look!' said Erik. 'Where there were thirty or forty of them before, it seems there are now three hundred – four hundred – maybe a thousand – see how their torches fill the mountainside!'

'Let us hope the Starsword has not lost its powers,' murmured Erik's men, 'for if it has, we are dead men.'

'It has its power still!' cried Thorkhild, and he stood there on the mountain top, with the Starsword held high above his head. 'But something is wrong … something is different …'

And the Starsword shook and glowed brighter and brighter until it was a white light, shining as if it were the sun itself, and none could look at it but had to turn their eyes away.

Then below them, they heard the roaring cease, and they looked down and saw, by the light of the Starsword, the monstrous creatures, with their heads in their chests, armed with mighty axes, spears and swords as long as the mast of Golden Dragon herself, but they were standing bewildered – dazzled by the light of the Starsword. Then a great clattering filled the air as the creatures let their weapons drop to the ground. And then the ground shook, as the monsters themselves fell upon their faces, covering the eyes in their chests, blinded by the Starsword.

'Now the Starsword will slay our enemies,' cried Erik's men, 'now that they are disarmed and disabled!'

But Thorkhild gave a cry of pain. 'It is different!' he shouted. 'The Starsword is burning in my hands!' But he held onto it, and the Starsword began to vibrate, and an unearthly note rose up from it, which began to change as the sword quivered faster and then slower and then faster again. And as it did so, note followed note, until they began to form a slow, haunting melody that enfolded the mountainside like a warm cloud.

'I cannot hold it much longer,' cried Thorkhild, 'for it burns my hands!'

'Quick!' said Erik. 'We must take our chance!'

'But we dare not move until the Starsword has slain each and every one of those terrible creatures!' cried his men.

But Thorkhild gave a great cry. 'Run!' he yelled. 'Run before the Starsword slays each and every one of us!' And at that, Erik set off down the mountainside towards the prostrate creatures. And although his men were filled with fear at the thought of running into the very midst of such an enemy, they saw nothing else for it and so they followed. Only Sven the Strong hung back.

'Run!' cried out Thorkhild. 'I cannot hold the sword much longer!'

But Sven the Strong did not run. Instead he bent and lifted the blind Thorkhild onto his shoulders and then made his way swiftly after the others – the Starsword still singing its strange song as Thorkhild held it high above his head.

Down they went towards the gigantic monsters, and without hesitating Erik began to pick his way through them, there where they lay in their hundreds, and not one moved nor raised a hand to stop him or any of his men, as long as Thorkhild held the Starsword above his head.

And now the song the Starsword sang seemed to take on words … strange, outlandish words that neither Erik nor any of his men could understand.

'Hurry!' cried Thorkhild, 'I cannot hold this fire in my hand any longer!' And Sven the Strong redoubled his efforts, threading his way through the fallen giants. Several times he stumbled and almost fell beneath his load, but he managed to keep going, until – just as they had reached the last of the prostrate monsters – Thorkhild gave a cry, and let go of the Starsword. Whereupon it flew out of his hand, and the vibration and the music stopped abruptly. And the moment it did so, the giant creatures stirred, and one by one they began to raise themselves up, and started to gaze around by the light of the Starsword as it hung in the air above them. For a moment it burnt even brighter than the sun, but then it began to flicker and fade, until it became but a glowing ember, which shot across the sky like a shooting star, and then disappeared over the distant horizon.

Erik and his men made their way after it as swiftly as ever they could, and behind them they heard the half-blinded giants blundering about in the darkness. And so, before the creatures could stop them, the comrades regained their ship, Golden Dragon, and had soon put a mile of water between themselves and the land where the sun goes at night.

Then Erik called his men together and held a council of war. Some said they should turn back and fight, and some said they should keep going and leave the land where the sun goes at night far behind them.

'We have found the prize that we have been seeking so long,' said Sven the Strong. 'We cannot give it up without a fight!'

'But however can we defeat an enemy so monstrous and so numerous?' cried Gunnar Longshanks, and some of Erik's men murmured in agreement, and cast fearful glances towards the land that now lay on the horizon.

Then Ragnar Forkbeard stood up and held aloft the golden moon that he had carried all the way back. 'Look!' he said, and he took hold of the moon, and pulled the two horns of the crescent so that it suddenly opened up.

Erik and his men crowded round to see what wonderful thing could be held in such a precious container. But when they looked into it, all they could see was earth.

'Wait!' said Ragnar Forkbeard, and he took a barleycorn from the ship's stores, and pushed it into the earth, and at once a tall blade of barley shot up and was ripe and ready for cutting. 'A land that holds such riches as this earth is not to be given up without a struggle. Are we all turned cowards that we are ready to give up the very thing we have been seeking, merely because we shall have to fight for it?'

At these words, the rest of Erik's men hung their heads in shame, and Erik said, 'There is only one way we can defeat such an enemy and gain such a prize ...' and he turned to Thorkhild who had stood by silent all this while.

'Thorkhild!' he said. 'You have not spoken, and you can often see things that others cannot, whether your eyes see them or no. Tell us: how can we regain the Starsword to help us to win this land?'

Thorkhild heaved a sigh, and replied, 'I do not know where the Starsword is to be found, and even if I did, I would dread to use it in this quest, for I fear that the Starsword would slay us before ever it helped us to win this land.'

'What do you mean?' cried Erik. 'Has it not already helped us?'

Then Thorkhild turned his blind eyes towards Erik, and said, 'It helped us to escape, but as I held the Starsword it burnt in my hands like fire, and its vibrations swept through my body and through my soul, and it seemed as if it were speaking to me through its song, and I could understand every word.'

'And what was the Starsword's song?' asked Erik.

'Its song was a warning,' said Thorkhild, 'that we are all as blind as I am now if we think of nothing but of possessing that land, and cannot see our true goal.'

'But surely! This is our true goal!' cried Erik's men.

'Not if the Starsword's song was true,' replied Thorkhild, 'for it sang of the deeds men do and the knowledge that those deeds are good – not of lands nor riches:

"Our deeds are our gold,

Our quest is our goal"

– these were its words.'

'I do not understand,' said Erik, 'for in our search we have been through many adventures – you and I and Ragnar Forkbeard and Sven the Strong and all the rest, and there has been courage unheard of and feats of arms, and always we have tried to do our best and

to do that which is right – even though at times it has been hard to know what that was.'

'Perhaps this is such a time,' replied Thorkhild, and he turned his blind face towards the black night across the sea and went on, 'Those monstrous creatures were indeed hideous to behold, and more terrible than any foe we have met before, and yet that does not make it right for us to kill them or to steal their land away from them.'

'But they would have killed us, if we had not defended ourselves first!' cried Erik.

'Who are we to say?' replied Thorkhild. 'For what was terrible roaring in our ears may have been words of friendship in their mouths. And for all we know that first awful creature, when it stretched out its fist above us may have been offering us a gift of friendship instead of threatening us … may have been giving us the golden moon, only we were too frightened to see.'

And Thorkhild put out his hands, and Ragnar Forkbeard placed the golden moon in them, and Thorkhild plucked the ear of barley and scattered its grains to the wind. As he did so, the seagulls that followed in the wake of the ship, pecked them out of the air, and at once turned into stars that flew up into the heavens, and became a constellation shaped like a woman, calling them across the seas.

Then Erik stood up, on board Golden Dragon, and said, 'We have been to the land where the sun goes at night … I may sleep in my bed again. But in finding that land, we almost lost ourselves. It is indeed a wonderful place, but this moonful of earth is all of it to which we have a right and all of it that we shall take.'

And with that, they set the sail of Golden Dragon towards home.

THE LAST TRICK

LONG AND WEARY was that last voyage of Golden Dragon. And many a time Erik and his men thought their last hours had come, what with giant waves and tempests and monsters of the deep. And many a time they wished themselves back safe on the shores of home.

But one morning, as dawn was breaking, they heard the look-out cry: 'Land ahead!' And they all crowded to the prow of Golden Dragon, and peered into the sea breeze, and there – sure enough – was a land of snow-capped mountains on the horizon.

'We are home!' cried Erik, and his men cheered, and they threw their helmets into the air. But before a single helmet had returned to the hand that threw it, they heard a noise of rushing water, and they looked to port and saw the sea rushing past them in the direction they were going.

'What is happening?' cried Erik's men. 'The sea is overtaking us!'

And just then they found themselves caught up in a headlong rush of waters, and suddenly the ship was being dragged away from the land, and they looked beyond and saw the sea rushing back in the opposite direction, and they realised it was swirling them round and round, and faster and faster they went in a circle.

'It's a whirlpool!' cried Erik. 'The Old Man of the Sea has not finished playing his tricks on us yet!'

And as they clung to the deck and the sea swung them around faster and faster, the centre of the whirlpool grew black and started to drop away below them, so that the ship Golden Dragon was now on a vertical wall of sea, being swept round and round.

Erik and his men clung on as best they could, and their hearts filled with despair, for they had seen their homeland on the horizon, only to be snatched away to face again the terrors of the deep. And Erik looked over the side of Golden Dragon and peered down into the depths of the whirlpool, which now was sucking them down as they span faster and faster. And he saw the terrible blackness of the deep, as the whirlpool opened up wider

and wider, and the funnel of water seemed to stretch for a mile below them. Still they spiralled down and down, and not one of them dared look up to see the frightful walls of water above them. Still the whirlpool yawned wider, until Ragnar Forkbeard gave a shout, and there was the sea-bed itself … the bottom of the ocean, exposed to the eye of day for the very first time!

'We have seen our home and the bottom of the sea in the space of time it takes an arrow to fly from the bowstring to the bull's-eye,' murmured Erik. 'Let us pray for some miracle that will take us back as quickly – for this time I do not know what else there is that we can do.'

But just then they heard a noise like thunder below them, even louder than the roaring of the whirlpool, and they looked down in wonder and saw the ocean bed itself opening up as if to receive them. And down they went into the very rock beneath the sea, and they heard it close up again above them, and for a moment they were in pitch darkness.

Neither Erik nor Ragnar Forkbeard nor Sven the Strong nor any of the others had the stomach to utter so much as a single sound. But the blind Thorkhild said, 'Dark or light makes no difference now to me … but I feel a fire burning somewhere in this dank coldness …'

'How can that be?' shivered Erik's men.

But Ragnar Forkbeard said, 'Wait! What is that?' and sure enough, they began to make out a glow in the pitch darkness coming from the stern of Golden Dragon. Ragnar Forkbeard ran towards it, and for a moment all went black again, but then he turned and they could see, lying upon his sword, a glowing ember.

'I do not know whether I dare to believe this,' whispered Erik. 'But can it be that the Starsword did not desert us after all – but fell here on board Golden Dragon and has lain hidden here ever since?'

'Give it to me,' said Thorkhild, and Ragnar Forkbeard passed the blade to him. Then the others brought lamps and candles and lit them from the glowing ember of the Starsword.

Now their flickering torches lit up the darkness beneath the sea bed, and they saw they were in a great chamber cut out of black rock, and there was a banqueting table and chairs all made of the same material. And at the far end of the chamber was a black throne, over which hung a canopy of black, and on the throne slouched a being – black from head to toe, with two beady yellow eyes glaring at them.

'Who or what is this?' whispered Erik's men, one to the other. 'Where are we?'

The black creature on the throne put out a black claw and beckoned to Erik.

Erik stepped forward, a burning torch in one hand, the other hand upon his sword. 'Who are you?' he said. But the slippery black being did not reply. Only its yellow eyes blinked once, and Erik felt strangely fearful in the pit of his stomach.

'What do you want with me?' he asked. But the black creature merely trickled to its feet like quicksilver poured into a phial, and once again beckoned to Erik. Then it turned and slid towards a door in the black chamber, and Erik followed, with one fearful glance back at his companions, who stood there beneath their torches and candles as if frozen to the spot.

As Erik stepped through the door he felt a gust of wind on his face, and it felt like the wind that blows the moon through the sky at night … an old wind … cold as the grave … and Erik shuddered. He found himself in a great high hall hung around with strange pictures – grim scenes of evil and destruction – and at the far end of the hall was a figure in a black cloak sitting at a game of chess …

'Don't go!' whispered a voice at his elbow, and Erik turned to find Ragnar Forkbeard gazing earnestly into his eyes. 'You cannot win against such an opponent.'

'I must go,' replied Erik. 'I accepted the challenge and now I must play one game of chess with Death.'

And at these words the black creature seemed to dissolve and pour itself like black treacle from a jar into a long streak that froze into a shining black walkway that ran the length of the great hall. And before Ragnar Forkbeard could stop him, Erik was striding along the ebony path towards that grim figure hunched over the chess board.

THE LAST TRICK

'I have come!' said Erik. 'Here I am to play with you when you will, Death.' And Erik stood there in the silence of the great hall under the sea bed, and waited as the figure rose and slowly turned to face him.

The moment it did so, Erik turned pale and his knees trembled. His head spun, and he felt a wind again upon his face – only this time it felt like the wind that blew on his face when he was a child, watching the great ships leave the harbour at Drangar in Hornstrands, and his mother was waving goodbye with tears in her eyes. For, although the face that turned upon him was thin and hollow as a skull, it was not Death.

'Can it be really you, Erik?' said a cracked voice.

And all Erik could say was, 'Yes, Father.'

BLUEBLADE

HOW LONG THEY STOOD there staring at each other, Erik and his father, I don't know. But sooner or later they embraced each other, and tears poured down their cheeks.

'We thought you were dead many, many years ago,' cried Erik.

'And so I should have been,' replied his father, 'for our ship was caught in a terrible tempest just when we were in sight of land, and was likely to have foundered with all on board, so I made a bargain with the Old Man of the Sea that I would come and keep him company beneath the waves, if he would spare the lives of my companions. But then he locked me in this dungeon, and I have dwelt here ever since. It has been a living death here beneath the ocean floor, and many times I cursed that day I made the deal, but there was nothing I could do, and nothing could release me – except one thing, and one thing only.'

'What was that?' asked Erik.

'You,' replied his father.

'Me?' said Erik.

'This was the Old Man of the Sea's curse: that I should languish here forever, unless my son should find the goal that all men seek. And I had little hope that the small child I had left behind with his mother on the harbour wall would ever discover such a thing, and so I resigned myself to an eternity of despair – yet now here you are!'

'But I have not found such a goal!' cried Erik.

Just then there was a cry from the door, and there stood Thorkhild … the blind Thorkhild … though his eyes seemed to be almost glowing with some strange light.

'But you have!' he cried. 'It is what we have all discovered during this long voyage. Do you not remember the Starsword's song?'

'I remember the Starsword's song,' said Erik, and he turned back to his father and said: 'When we set sail, we thought we were seeking the land where the sun goes at night, but when we got there we found it wasn't what we were searching for at all …'

'And so often it is the case,' replied his father. 'We find that our true goal lies within ourselves and in what we do, and not in the things we think we are looking for.'

The ember of the Starsword seemed to glow redder as he spoke, and Erik replied, 'Then the Starsword's song was true: our quest has been our goal ...'

At these words there was a sound of oceans rushing together, and there stood the Old Man of the Sea in a swirling pillar of water, seething with rage.

'Erik the Viking!' he cried, waving his arm with its missing hand, 'You have tricked me twice before, but you shall not trick me a third time! You think you'll save your father, do you? Very well, you shall ... but beware! For if you take him away from me, your men, Erik, shall stay to keep me company! And whichever of them tries to pass back through my kingdom of the icy waters shall perish!'

And as he spoke a swirling wall of water shot up between Erik and his father, and another between Erik and Thorkhild and Ragnar Forkbeard and the others.

'The choice is yours!' screamed the Old Man of the Sea, and he laughed a laugh like an ocean storm, and the pillar of water poured itself up into the ceiling of the hall, and the Old Man of the Sea was gone too.

Then Erik stood alone in his dilemma, turning over in his mind the choice before him. What should he do? Should he save his father, who had lain beneath the bottom of the sea so long, and let his comrades perish? Or save his comrades and leave his father in despair for eternity.

'Do not hesitate!' shouted Erik's father. 'I am but one man — save your comrades!'

'But we can help each other!' shouted Ragnar Forkbeard, from behind the other wall of water. 'Save your father, and we'll find some way out!'

But Erik turned from one to the other and said, 'I shall not leave this hideous place without each and every one of you.' And he put his hand to his hip and drew his sword, Blueblade. 'The Old Man of the Sea can stop us returning back, up through his kingdom of the icy waters if he wants,' cried Erik, 'but he shall not keep us imprisoned in this dungeon here.'

'But how can we escape unless we return back up through his kingdom of the icy waters?' cried Erik's men. 'There is no other way.'

'There is one way!' said Erik. 'Thorkhild, throw me the Starsword.'

And Thorkhild threw the glowing ember through the wall of water, and as it flew it seemed to burn a hole in the waterwall. Then Erik quickly thrust the tip of Blueblade into the ember so that it stuck fast, and then he held Blueblade aloft, with the point glowing. And then it was that a most marvellous thing happened … the glowing ember seemed to burn brighter and fiercer than ever, and Blueblade began to tremble in Erik's hand, and they heard a note — the same as they had heard when the Starsword had sung its song. And then Blueblade itself began to glow, and the note got louder and clearer and it seemed as if the ember then melted into Erik's sword, and the two became one.

'Erik!' cried Thorkhild. 'For a brief moment I held the most wonderful sword in my hands, and then I knew I could achieve that which I ought to achieve, but now my eyes are stones that see only endless night, and that power shall never again be mine. But look, Erik, you who can see, for I hear by that song that is now ringing in my ears that the Starsword is now yours. Erik, the Starsword has become your sword, Blueblade!'

BLUEBLADE

At these words, Erik smote the rock floor beneath the two walls of water, so that a crevice opened up beneath each one, and the water poured away down it. Then Erik took his sword, Blueblade, and struck the wall of the chamber, and the sword embedded itself up to the hilt in the solid rock. As the companions watched, they saw the handle of Blueblade turning, as if a huge invisible hand were cutting a large circle in the rock. As the sword completed the circle, the rock within it crumbled into dust, and a wind swept through the chamber and blew it into a mist so that no one could see for a few moments.

When the mist settled, they saw Blueblade had disappeared down a long tunnel it was cutting itself through the solid rock of the sea bed.

'We cannot return up through the Old Man of the Sea's kingdom of the icy waves,' said Erik, 'but down here in this rock he has no power. This is our way home.'

And he led his father and his companions down the tunnel that Blueblade cut and, in the distance, high above them, they heard the Old Man of the Sea roaring with rage, for he had been out-witted for the third time.

HOW ERIK RETURNED HOME

AND SO ERIK AND his men returned home, following the tunnel that Blueblade cut under the sea-bed and then up to the surface. And when at last they stepped up into the sunlight, and saw that they were indeed on the shore of their own land, they kissed the ground, and gave thanks that they had returned – safe after so many adventures.

In the distance they saw smoke curling up from over a hill, and Erik's father said, 'Is that the very village I left so long ago?' and the tears came to his eyes. And as they looked they could hear – faintly in the distance – the early morning sounds of the village awakening … cows lowing, dogs barking … and each of them laughed inside himself with joy to think of the surprise and happiness that they would bring with their arrival.

So without more ado they set off towards their home, but they had taken no more than a couple of steps when Erik stopped dead in his tracks.

'Let's hurry!' cried Sven the Strong. 'I cannot wait to see how my children have grown!'

But Ragnar Forkbeard looked at Erik and asked: 'What is it, Erik?'

'Is it him?' whispered the blind Thorkhild.

'Yes,' said Erik, and he pointed to a dark figure sitting upon a rocky crag that overhung the wild sea. 'Death is waiting for his game of chess.'

Then the comrades clustered around Erik. They begged him at least to show himself at home, before he went to meet Death. But Erik turned away from them, and said, 'I must go. I have no choice.'

'Nobody can win a single game against Death,' cried Sven the Strong. 'Don't go, Erik!' But Erik was already striding across the shore towards the rocky crag where Death sat waiting.

'Here I am, Death,' said Erik. And Death turned the board so that the white pieces were in front of Erik.

'Are you not frightened of losing?' asked Death.

'I am not afraid of you,' said Erik. 'And whether I win or lose, I enjoy a game of chess – so let us begin!' And he moved a white pawn, and Death moved his queen's knight.

So they played, with the sea pounding against the crag below them, and the wind racing onto the shore and off towards the wild mountains that hung above them. And the sun climbed high into the sky, while Erik's companions waited and watched from the distance. The sea roared and the wind blew, and still Erik and Death sat at their game on that rocky crag. Then the sun began to slip away towards the West, and still Erik and Death sat and played at chess.

'Erik cannot win against such an opponent,' grieved Erik's father. But Thorkhild said, 'Let us wait and see.'

Just then Death took one of Erik's pawns, and looked into Erik's eyes, and said, 'Why do you play against me? You know you cannot win.'

And Erik replied, 'I enjoy a game of chess. I'll play against anyone who'll play me,' and he took Death's castle.

Death looked angry, and there was a rumble of thunder on the horizon, and Erik thought he could hear the wolves of Wolf Mountain howling far across the seas.

'I am Death,' said Erik's opponent. 'Everyone lives in fear of me.'

'You are wrong,' said Erik. 'To me you are like an old friend, and I've been quite looking forward to this little game,' and he took Death's other castle.

The sky went dark, and the thunder roared all along the shore, and echoed back against the mountains, and Erik thought, for a moment, he heard the gulls calling to each other as he had in the Talking Valley, and for another moment he thought he heard the ocean booming as it struck the crag, saying, 'You cannot win!' And the mountains echoed, 'Win! Win! Win!'

'I am Death,' said Erik's opponent. 'All men are at my beck and call, and every man must come as and when I choose.'

'Nonsense!' said Erik. 'A man may choose death at any instant he wants – for example, I have only to step off this crag if I choose – I do not need you to call me!' and he took Death's bishop.

Then a flash of lightning streaked across the sky, and seemed to strike the very mountains, and the crash of thunder drowned the roaring of the sea, and Erik's men shivered with fear as the rain began to fall upon them.

And then Death took Erik's queen, and said, 'None shall escape me, Erik … neither you nor your father nor your men. Each and every one of you shall be mine. And nothing of you shall remain – do you hear – nothing!'

And Erik felt a shudder of cold go through his body as he stared at the board, but, even as he did, he heard a voice say, 'You are wrong!'

Erik looked up and the breath left his body, and his heart stopped beating for an instant, as if Death were already snatching at him. But he blinked and looked again, and there sure enough was a third figure standing beside them on the rocky crag.

For a moment he thought it was his father grown miraculously young who was standing there. But it was not his father. The figure laughed, and as he laughed Erik suddenly recognised the fifteen-year-old son he had left behind so long ago, who had grown – while Erik was away – into a man.

'Death, you old fool!' said the boy. 'Have you forgotten that I am Erik's son, and though you may take him, I shall remain!'

'I shall have you too!' snarled Death. 'For I hold dominion over Life itself!'

'No, you don't,' replied Erik's son, 'for when I am gone, my son shall remain and then my son's son and then his son and then his and then his … You may do what you want, Death, but you cannot destroy Life itself!'

And with that Death rose to his feet, knocked the chess board over so that the pieces scattered upon the crags, and turned to Erik, and growled, 'We shall finish our game another time, you and I.' There was a clap of thunder and a flash of lightning, and Death was gone. And Erik looked over the crag, and saw the chequered board floating on the wild waves below.

Then Erik embraced his son, and his father and his comrades gathered round, and together they returned home to the place where they were born.

When they arrived, Erik kissed his wife a thousand times, and she him. And his mother was reunited with his father.

Then Erik called everyone together and spoke: 'We have faced the Dragon of the North Sea, we have three times tricked the Old Man of the Sea, we have been turned to stone, we have fought the Dogfighters, we have travelled across bitter snows, we have crossed Wolf Mountain, we have faced spirits and trolls, and the great bird of doubt, we have heard the Talking Valley, and we have been to the edge of the world and over it, we have visited the Secret Lake, and we have found the land where the sun goes at night … And all we have brought back are these four gifts of air, fire, earth and water …

'The first is water,' he said, and handed the giant's jug to his wife. 'Now we shall never go thirsty again. The second is earth.' And he handed the golden moon to his father, and said: 'With the wonderful earth in this moon we shall never go hungry again. The third is fire,' he said, and he drew his sword, Blueblade, and handed it to his son, saying, 'This has been my sword, now it is yours, and with it – as long as justice and truth are by your side – you will protect us from every enemy.' Then Erik's son held Blueblade high above his head, and the Starsword within started to sing, and it glowed like fire.

'The fourth gift is a poor one,' said Erik, 'but I give to you all, for it is the breath in my body, and as long as I have it I shall use it on your behalf.'

Then they lit a great fire in memory of Golden Dragon, that still lay beneath the bottom of the ocean, and they pledged themselves to build a new ship as soon as winter was past.

Then they celebrated with a feast. And long into the night Erik and his men took turns to tell these stories that you have just been listening to.

THE END

ALSO AVAILABLE

BY TERRY JONES AND MICHAEL FOREMAN

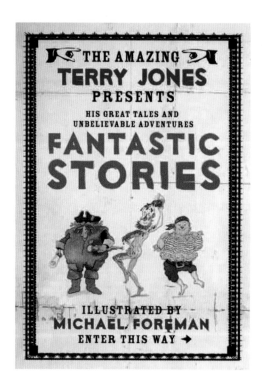

The Fantastic World of Terry Jones:
Fantastic Stories (9781843651628)

ALSO AVAILABLE
BY MICHAEL FOREMAN

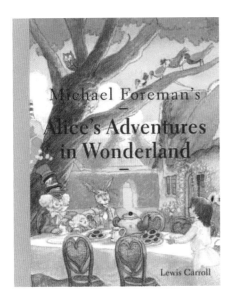

Michael Foreman's Alice's
Adventures in Wonderland
(9781843653080)

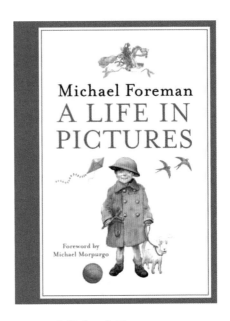

Michael Foreman:
A Life in Pictures
(9781843652991)

War Game
(9781843651789)